Jardun's Embrace

RAYNA TYLER

ISBN: 978-1-953213-00-6

ALSO BY RAYNA TYLER

Seneca Falls Shifters

Tempting the Wild Wolf
Captivated by the Cougar
Enchanting the Bear
Enticing the Wolf
Teasing the Tiger

Ketaurran Warriors

Jardun's Embrace
Khyron's Claim
Zaedon's Kiss
Rygael's Reward
Logan's Allure
Garyck's Gift

Crescent Canyon Shifters

Engaging His Mate
Impressing His Mate

Bradshaw Bears

Bear Appeal

CHAPTER ONE

LARIA

The assignment is simple. I need you to retrieve a package. Those were the last and only instructions I'd received from Burke before making the half-day journey to Aztrashar, one of the few remaining inhabitable cities on Ketaurrios.

It hadn't taken me long once I reached my destination to discover that nothing about his request was simple. Not the location, not the three luzardees, one of the planet's humanoid reptile species, and certainly not what I'd assumed was the "package."

Shortly after entering what I considered to be one of the worst excuses for a bar I'd ever seen, I surveyed the interior. The five-year war, a result of a sibling's attempt to overthrow his brother's rule, had left its devastating mark on the planet, this place included. Now that it was over, the survivors, human and ketaurran alike, were doing their best to rebuild their lives out of what was left. Apparently, the owner of the establishment didn't fall into that category.

If I thought the outside of the building was bad, with its thin cracks, randomly scorched walls, and numerous chunks missing from the reddish-brown adobe-like exterior, the inside wasn't much better. The place had been stripped of everything except the barest amount of furniture. It reeked of stale ale, body odor, and urine. I'd bet the handful of cradasson coins I had stuffed in my pocket that the place hadn't been cleaned in days, possibly weeks.

Out-of-the-way locations like this one had become the preferred meeting place when dealing with lowlife, cutthroat mercs, bounty chasers, or thieves. I was certain, from their arrogant demeanor and hardened expressions, that these particular males qualified as all three.

Life wasn't exactly easy, and there were those who spent their time using alcoholic liquids to temporarily dull their horrible memories, to make their existence easier to deal with. I was a little surprised to find the place lacking in patrons. Other than the luzardees, a balding middle-aged human male with hairy arms and a paunchy midsection was the only other person in the room. He stood behind a long serving counter attentively paying attention, yet seemed uninterested in my presence. No one in the room had been served a drink, nor did they act as if they were expecting one.

"Are you lost, female?" the luzardee seated at the table closest to me asked. He'd been staring at me as if I were a delectable feast from the moment I'd entered the room.

No, I wasn't lost, but I was definitely reconsidering my decision to come inside alone. Beneath his animal hide vest and pants, his body was covered in one endless sheet of hairless tan scales. He glared at me with beady black eyes that lacked pupils, and flared the nostrils on his flat face. Of the three, he was the tallest and the biggest, which wasn't saying much since his lanky frame wasn't much wider than mine.

Tiny white flecks clung to portions of his scaly skin, a sign he'd been spending too much time in the sun, or he was getting ready to go through his yearly shedding.

Whichever it was made my skin itch, and I fought the urge to scratch my arm.

Now that I was here, leaving wasn't an option. "I'm looking for someone named Kowhl."

A slight squint was all the indication I needed to know I'd found the person I'd been sent here to meet.

"I am Kowhl. What is the nature of your businesss?" He leered even more.

I'd learned from my past interactions with the luzardees that they spoke with a slight lisp, which only became more prominent when they were anxious or excited. The way his gaze kept dropping to my cleavage told me it was the latter.

I gave the door an inconspicuous glance, questioning for the third time in the last ten minutes what had happened to my backup. And by backup, I meant Celeste and Sloane. They were my traveling companions, my closest friends, and the only two women on the entire planet who were closer to me than sisters. But no matter how much we discussed our plans ahead of time, they were always, always, always…late.

I straightened my shoulders and pushed aside my disgust. "Burke sent me."

The luzardee's pause was brief, his disappointed gaze replaced by a greedy gleam. "Sit." He angled his head toward the seat across the table from him.

I preferred to keep my distance, but sitting would make reaching the knife in my boot easier if things headed in a bad direction. I silently cursed my friends for being late one more time to make myself feel better, then cautiously pulled out the chair. I was hesitant to take a seat, not because the furniture lacked cleanliness, but because the chair appeared unstable. The loud creak I heard when I sat only reinforced my observation.

Kowhl glanced at the man behind the counter. "Leave us."

With a nod, the barkeep headed for a doorway leading

to the back of the building. Chances were he'd been compensated in advance for the use of his bar.

I thought about Burke's parting words again and wondered what he'd gotten my friends and me into. "Burke said I was supposed to retrieve a package."

I accepted all the intricacies that came along with my association with Burke because they kept me fed and prevented me from living out of a trash recycler. Something I'd had to do more than once and preferred never to do again.

Burke was military to his core. He'd led one of the security details assigned to the *Starward Bounty*. The exploration spaceship from Earth had carried nearly three hundred people: scientists, agriculturists, and their families. It had been my home for over a year before it was forced way off course by a bizarre meteor storm, then crash-landed on Ketaurrios.

Several years after we'd settled on the planet, the war had started and changed our lives forever. During and after those dreadful times, Burke led a group of rebels who did their best to protect the surviving humans. The man could be devious, ruthless when necessary, and sometimes showed a disregard for decent morals. All qualities I'd witnessed on numerous occasions and, in current times, understood why they were necessary.

I trusted him, at least with my life. And in that regard, I owed him a debt. A debt I'd never be able to repay, so here I was, ready to collect whatever he wanted, no questions asked. Correction: I had questions, a few of them, and would make sure to ask them later. If I'd been in the same room with Burke and not discussing the retrieval via my vehicle's less than adequate sometimes-staticky communication unit, I would've taken the time to gather more information.

I'd done quite a few jobs for him over the years, some dangerous and some I'd been aware stretched or jumped way over the fine line defining some of the planet's laws.

This was one of those rare times when I wanted to kick myself for not getting more details.

I'd been tagged with the role of acquisition specialist, a glamorous way of saying I acquired things or performed tasks most people wouldn't risk doing, so others could stay alive. When Burke used the term "package," I'd expected something the size of a small box at most, a large crate containing food, supplies, or maybe some stolen blades.

Even if I'd used my imagination, I never would have expected the package to be a man. Or rather male, since all the species, other than humans of that specific gender, insisted they be referred to by the latter.

Not that any of that mattered. At the moment, my objective was getting my package and myself out of here without either of us getting injured.

Without taking my attention off Kowhl, I glanced at the male sitting in the corner with his wrists and ankles shackled in chains. The majority of his body was covered with a hooded coat. Judging by his massive shoulders and the pale green tint of his exposed skin, I was pretty sure he was a ketaurran.

I'd lived on the planet long enough to learn the customs and history of its inhabitants. Unlike the animal-based evolution on Earth, the alien species on Ketaurrios evolved from a lizard-type ancestry. Surprisingly, most of them were warm-blooded. The ketaurrans were the predominant race. Though a portion of their body was covered with smooth scales, their anatomy was humanoid, including their reproductive systems. Relationships between the ketaurrans and humans were rare, but they did exist and occasionally resulted in children.

My suspicions were confirmed when I glimpsed his long, pointed tail swish across the floor near his booted feet. Just because his face was partially hidden didn't mean I couldn't feel his penetrating gaze focused on me. It wasn't my fault he was in chains, so I wasn't sure why I'd become the focus of his scrutiny.

If his intent was intimidation, it wasn't working. I'd been in enough difficult situations and many hours of hand-to-hand combat training, courtesy of Burke and some of the other guys who worked with him, to let one male bother me.

As far as the planet's technology went, the inhabitants didn't utilize their resources to create any kind of advanced weaponry. Traveling wasn't always safe, and some of the places my friends and I visited were dangerous. Being able to protect ourselves was a normal part of our lives. With knives and swords the weapons of choice, one could say there wasn't a blade on the planet that I couldn't wield with the precision of an assassin.

I was more concerned with being stuck in the middle of a situation that had the potential for going bad on so many levels. Besides being outnumbered by the luzardees, I wondered what kind of problems I'd encounter before I got the prisoner to Burke. If things went wrong and he decided his captors were less of a threat than I was, I might have more trouble than I could handle. There was always a possibility that the ketaurran had friends. Friends who might be looking for him, might not be happy the luzardees had captured him, or who might view me as a threat.

Since the male was shackled with heavy chains, I wasn't too worried about transporting him. Ketaurrans weren't easily subdued. It was hard to imagine any scenario where this guy would allow himself to be captured, especially by the two luzardees hovering close to him.

Remaining calm and hoping Celeste and Sloane made a timely appearance was all I could do at the moment.

"My payment," Kowhl demanded.

I pulled a pouch of coins from my pocket and dropped it on the table.

The luzardee glanced at the bag, then back at me. "I wish to renegotiate. It will cost you an additional fifty cradasson before I release him to you."

Slimy lizard. I had great instincts and should have listened to them a lot sooner. The niggle of dread, a definite warning that things were about to go wrong, exploded at the base of my neck and shot along my spine with an irritating intensity. "Look, I'm just the retrieval person." I returned his glare, refusing to show any signs of weakness.

"If you want more money, you'll need to take it up with Burke." I suppressed the urge to finger the handle of the blade tucked tightly against my calf. "Though you might want to know the last guy who tried to change the terms of his negotiation hasn't walked right for a long time." Actually, the guy had only limped for a week, but I wasn't above twisting the truth if it meant I'd get out of here without losing any of my body parts.

The luzardee standing closest to the prisoner smacked the long handle of a stun stick against his scaly palm and four digits. Without provocation, he jabbed one end of the stick into the prisoner's ribs. I heard an electrical crackle and watched tiny bolts of blue and yellow fly from the tip.

The chains dangling from the cuffs around the ketaurran's wrists were tethered to another set of cuffs attached around his ankles. He growled, and the chains rattled and jerked to a stop inches before he could grab the stick. The shock from the stick was painful, and a normal person would have been screaming by now. It took someone with a lot of strength and endurance to withstand that kind of pain.

Seriously, did the jerk think hurting the male was going to change my mind? Though I'd seen my share of torture and didn't get squeamish at the sight, it didn't mean I was a fan. "Could you stop tormenting my prisoner?" The damn lizards could smell even the slightest change in emotion, so I forced myself to remain calm and kept my voice as nonchalant as possible.

"Why do you care what we do to him?" Kowhl wiggled his nostrils and widened the lid on one of his reptilian eyes.

"I don't." I leaned back in my chair and crossed my arms, masking my features with indifference. "Burke will, though. He won't appreciate having to explain to whoever placed the bounty on this guy's head how the burn marks ended up all over his body. It wouldn't surprise me if you got a visit from some of his men." As I'd hoped, the threat got the desired results. Kowhl jerked his head at the other male, silently ordering him to stop.

I scooted my chair back. "I need to get going, so if you'll…" He grabbed my wrist, keeping me in my seat.

"Sssstay." He released his grip and ran one of his four clawlike fingertips along the back of my hand. "I have never had an Earther female. You can keep Burke's coins if you provide me with an afternoon of pleasure."

Bile crept along the back of my throat, leaving a nasty taste in my mouth. I swallowed several times, forcing it back to my stomach. I'd heard the luzardees had male parts similar to a human's, but it didn't mean I wanted a firsthand view. As far as I was concerned, there was nothing on the planet, including coins, that would ever make me want to sell my body. I wasn't about to be his first anything and was happy to disappoint him.

I had a feeling his idea of an afternoon of pleasure included his friends. If they hadn't been interested in our conversation before, they definitely were paying attention now. The male standing on Kowhl's right swiped his forked tongue along his bottom lip, no doubt anticipating where he wanted to use it. If a pair of beady eyes could reflect lustful desires, then these guys were practically glowing with it.

Most of the males I came in contact with weren't the relationship kind, and jumping into bed with a male just to satisfy a need wasn't usually my thing. Neither was sharing.

This situation was getting way beyond uncomfortable, and waiting for Celeste and Sloane to arrive wasn't helping. One way or another, I was leaving. It was either going to be easy, in which case I walked out with my package, or hard and bloody, with large amounts of bodily harm—preferably not mine.

I was leaning toward easy, but a part of me would enjoy hard just so I could teach Kowhl a lesson in manners. Doing my best to hide my revulsion, I pulled my hand away from his. "Sorry, I work for Burke, and he has strict rules about those kinds of things." I inched my hand toward the top of my boot. "And, as I stated before, it's *never* a good idea to cross him."

The ketaurran, who'd remained silent while he warily watched my interaction with the luzardees, released a low, predatory growl that sounded a lot like a wild animal. He shook his head back and forth, the hood dropping away and exposing his face. Obsidian strands draped along prominent cheekbones, the longer lengths tucked behind his head. His intense dark gaze flared with jade, his focus pinned on Kowhl.

Surprisingly, I didn't startle or share the same fear-filled expression as the luzardees. Instead, my stomach fluttered and warmth spread through my entire body. I couldn't remember the last time I'd found a male so devastatingly handsome, or had such a strong reaction. I forced myself to remember where I was and what I needed to do. I used the distraction to push out of the chair and position myself closer to the door.

Before the luzardee could shock the ketaurran again, the bartender walked into the room. "Hey, there won't be no problems inside my establishment." He warned through gritted teeth. "It's bad for business."

No one had left or entered the place since I'd arrived, so I wasn't sure what business he was referring to. I got a little nervous when he reached underneath the bar's scarred and worn wooden counter to retrieve an antiquated blaster. I hadn't seen one of them in years. They weren't exactly legal back on Earth, and the few humans who still owned one had smuggled them onto the ship in their personal belongings.

The weapon, courtesy of a poor engineering design, lacked any decent targeting capabilities. Not a requirement if the user's goal was to hit anything in the general vicinity of where they were aiming. It wasn't designed to kill, more like stun, but could do some serious damage to those who were standing close when it was fired. If I remembered correctly, they were also notorious for occasionally backfiring, causing injury to the person who pulled the trigger—a fact I hoped the bartender was aware of.

I glanced from the bartender's serious frown to the Kowhl's irritated glare and tried to decide if he thought bending me over a table was worth having a majority of his scales ripped from his body.

"No problemsss here." He slowly got to his feet, taking a few steps backward.

"Glad to hear it." The bartender lowered his weapon, but was smart enough not to put it away.

I gave him an appreciative nod, then spoke to Kowhl. "If you'll unchain his feet, we'll be leaving now." I pointed at the ketaurran, then glanced toward the dirt-coated pane of the window near the exit. There was still no sign of Celeste and Sloane. I inhaled a calming breath before my frustration could reach the ready-to-throttle-them mode.

"Do as she asksss." Kowhl's lisp was getting worse, his scaly cheeks flushing a dark green.

The ketaurran was yanked to his feet. One luzardee held the stun stick inches from his chest, while the other unlocked the shackles binding his legs and removed them from his ankles. Once the chains clanked to the floor, the prisoner was shoved in my direction.

I kept my back to the door, then turned to my prisoner. "Let's go." I was two inches shy of six feet, yet the ketaurran towered over me by at least four inches. He offered no resistance when I placed my hand on the firm, thick muscles above his elbow and urged him toward the door. I stayed by his side, moving backwards, my gaze leveled at the three males and their hateful glares.

Unless I knew them personally, I knew better than to trust any of Burke's associates. The luzardees had their payment, but it didn't stop my finely honed instincts for detecting trouble from blaring. I planned to put some distance between us and them as quickly as possible.

Once we were outside, I gripped the ketaurran's forearm and aimed him in the direction I wanted to go. Beneath the fabric of his coat, the man definitely had a set of muscles. It was impossible to curl my fingers around his arm. If he decided to struggle, I was going to end up bruised. "Do us both a favor and don't give me any problems." I split my attention between glancing over my shoulder and watching his reaction.

"The thought had not crossed my mind." His chuckle was not what I'd expected. Some growling, a smart-mouthed comment or two, maybe, but not the husky laugh that touched my feminine parts and made me shudder with warmth. Then there was the way he continually sniffed the air when he thought I wasn't looking. Ketaurrans had an enhanced sense of smell, and I wondered why he'd be committing mine to memory.

CHAPTER TWO

JARDUN

A draecking female. Did Burke not understand the seriousness of my request? What kind of game was the human male playing by sending a female to retrieve me?

I was certain the instructions I had sent him were clear. I was in need of assistance, preferably in the form of other males, armed males, males capable of surviving in battle should it become necessary. At the very least, I had expected Burke to make an appearance. Not this lone yet beautiful creature with golden hair and eyes that shimmered the deep green of a midday sky.

My relationship with the rebel leader began several years ago when our paths crossed during the war. We'd battled the enemy together in our attempt to help survivors. At times, his ethics were questionable, but he had never given me a reason to question his decision-making abilities or his loyalty. I believed I could rely on him for assistance with my latest mission. A secretive mission that required humans with strong fighting abilities and a special talent for procuring items without permission. At least I thought his assistance was a good choice, until I heard the female tell the luzardees she'd been sent to retrieve me on Burke's behalf.

After the war, my role as a vryndarr, an elite warrior who protected the drezdarr, the leader of my people, had changed. Now my team spent a lot of our time tracking down mercenaries and traitorous soldiers who were loyal to Sarus, the old king's younger brother and the male responsible for starting the war. The unsuccessful battle for power had cost many lives. Though our numbers were fewer, we continued to fight the internal battle to bring safety and harmony to all the inhabitants on Ketaurrios.

My current predicament was a result of that new role and one of my own making. Had I not been traveling alone and focused on my task, I would not have been foolish enough to walk into the trap the luzardee had set. I also would not have woken to find myself shackled and being traded for a bag of coins.

My level of frustration was pushed even higher when the luzardee prodded me with his stun stick. The display for the female was one of many I'd endured over the last few hours. Had I not been bound with chains, I would have broken the shackles and ripped the stick from the puny male's claws.

There were very few things on Ketaurrios that could be used to subdue a male such as me. The shackles made from the brugoran ore, retrieved from the depths beneath the Geborraan Mountains, binding my wrists and ankles, was one of them.

I could not reveal my true identity or the reason that led to my capture. The life of my friend, the future of my people as well as hers, depended on it. I had no other option than to remain silent and allow the female to demonstrate her abilities. Abilities I could neither fathom nor believe existed. It was more likely I would have to rescue her, then display my discontent on Burke with a few well-placed punches.

I was not easily impressed, but would admit the female

handled herself well and was gifted when it came to masking her emotions. The luzardees might have accepted her explanation for discontinuing the torture, but I had not missed her slight cringe or the brief distress that flashed in her alert gaze. No female, not even one of my own species, set my emotions aflame the way one concerned glance from this human had.

The growl that rumbled from my chest had been unexpected and had not helped my cause. The overwhelming need to protect was a response triggered the instant Kowhl had grabbed her wrist. Unlike the luzardees, she had shown no fear, not of the three males who leered at her, and not of me.

In that moment, shackled or not, I was prepared to tear the place apart if any of them touched her. Fortunately, the bartender's timely reappearance prevented my interference and assisted with our departure.

Once we were outside and away from the bar's stench, I got a whiff of her scent. Of all my senses, my enhanced smelling ability was my greatest asset. The enticing floral scent combined with her feminine aroma had my cock standing at attention and pressing uncomfortably against the confines of my pants. Though the heat radiating from my core and heating my entire body made wearing the hooded overcoat unnecessary, I was thankful I had worn it. Not only was it useful for concealing blades, it hid the evidence of my arousal.

In order to get close to her, I needed her to believe I was not a threat. It took every ounce of my concentration to focus on the plan instead of spending time exploring my attraction to her. "If you release me, I will ensure that you are heavily compensated."

She kept her hand on my arm and continued to move at a rapid pace toward a destination she had yet to share. I recognized the calculated glances she continually tossed over her shoulder, the assessment of her surroundings and how best to utilize them. My fellow ketaurrans and I used the same technique when we found ourselves in similar situations.

Was there more to this female than I had originally assumed? Was it possible she was aware that the luzardee could not be trusted, that they still posed a threat?

"Even if you had any coins, which I'm certain you don't, you can keep them. I'm not for sale." She huffed indignantly, jutting out her chin. "I've been instructed to deliver you, and that's exactly what I'm going to do. Whatever trouble you got yourself into is none of my business. You can discuss the terms of your release when we rendezvous with Burke."

Her tone was laced with sincerity, and it was obvious Burke had not shared the nature of my request. I was impressed with her response and pressed my lips together tightly to prevent a grin. The female had honor, a rare trait to go along with her fiery spirit, another addition to the list mounting in her favor. Ketaurran males, those trained to be warriors, were formidable. Most females, especially humans, found us intimidating and preferred to keep their distance. She continued to show no fear, only wariness for our surroundings. Something else that greatly appealed to me.

"This way." She tightened her grip and guided me into a wide passageway between two buildings.

We'd attracted some frowns and inquisitive stares from a few of the locals, a mixture of humans and natives alike, who were venturing along the city walkways. It would have been wiser to remain within the crowds, yet she'd chosen a less safe route. I wondered if she was aware of how easily I could overpower her.

We were halfway down the passageway when Kowhl stepped from the shadows. He moved to the center of the walkway. "Going somewhere?" He now carried the stun stick and was smacking it against his palm.

"Damn lizards. I knew they were going to be trouble," she mumbled, then shot me an apologetic glance. "Sorry, no offense."

"I had not taken one." Normally, the comparison of an inhabitant from my planet with a lower reptilian one from hers was considered an insult. The fact that she cared about my interpretation spoke to her character. Not all Earthers who had been stranded here after their space vessel crashed nearly a decade ago held a high opinion of my people. It did not matter that the humans had been welcomed and assisted with making Ketaurrios their home; there was still a minority who hated my species.

It did not help that the humans had been pulled into Sarus's war a few years after their arrival. He might not have succeeded, but the long years following his initial attack had taken many lives, destroyed many families. Not only had he targeted other ketaurrans, he had gone after humans as well. He showed no mercy, no willingness to spare females and children. The devastation was great, and many were still trying to recover from it.

LARIA

"I have changed my mind about my current agreement with Burke." Kowhl remained at the end of the passageway exit, blocking our path. He was far enough away that he had to raise his voice to be heard. I returned his sneer with a glare, wishing this had been one of those times when my instincts were wrong.

Besides the handful of human mercenaries I'd encountered after the war, the luzardees were at the top of the list for the most untrustworthy creatures on the planet. I knew ducking between the buildings wasn't the best plan, but the ketaurran was drawing too much attention. If I ended up in a fight with the luzardees, I wanted to ensure that no innocent bystanders were harmed.

"How so?" I asked, knowing I wasn't going to like his answer.

"I believe he will pay more if your return is part of the

negotiations." His sneer puckered his scaly lips and was all kinds of creepy.

Kowhl's earlier proposition raced through my mind, making me question if he still planned to collect on the pleasure thing, with or without my permission. Even so, I laughed. "You obviously don't know Burke. He doesn't renegotiate, not ever."

"That isss too bad. There are others who will pay for a human female to warm their beds." His tongue slipped out, the end rapidly twitching. "Unless I decide to keep you for myself."

"Burke is not going to be happy you detained us. Are you sure you're willing to risk getting on his bad side?" I shifted sideways to check the direction the ketaurran and I had traveled. "Now, where are the other two?" I muttered to myself, not expecting an answer, especially not from my prisoner. He'd be seeking freedom, and now would be a great opportunity for him to escape. Instead, he raised his gaze, alerting me to the other two males who were using the claws on the their hands and feet to move along the rough exterior of the buildings on either side of us. Their slow and steady movements were synchronized. Once they made it to the roof, they could crawl along the wall until they reached us.

Draeck. The luzardees might resemble humans to some extent, but they were still part lizard and possessed climbing abilities similar to an Earth reptile. Worse, they could launch themselves through the air from considerable heights, making it difficult to fight them.

I kept my voice low so only the ketaurran could hear me. "I don't suppose you know if these guys have any additional friends lurking around, do you?" Kowhl still hadn't moved and appeared to be waiting for the other two to attack and do all the work.

He kept his gaze on the luzardees moving in their direction. "Not that I am aware." He sounded sincere, no fluctuation in his voice that would make me think he was being untruthful.

I was good at reading people, but if I was wrong about him, and there were other luzardees in their crew, then we were definitely in trouble. Taking on three males would be difficult, but it wasn't the first time I'd been in a fight where the odds weren't in my favor, and I was determined to make sure it wasn't my last.

I lifted the hem at the back of my shirt, grazed the horizontal sheath attached to my pants, and withdrew the short, thin blade. In my opinion, displaying weapons until they were needed gave your opponent an advantage. Having easy access was also a plus. It was the reason I kept my weapons hidden, and in more than one place on my body.

His eyes widened when he saw my blade and realized what I planned to do with it. I knew he was shocked. Women on Ketaurrios didn't fight, at least not the ketaurran ones. In their culture, the males were trained for battle and were required to protect them.

His disbelief turned into a frown. "I can be of more help if you remove my bindings." He held out his cuffed and chained wrists.

My trust had to be earned. "I appreciate the offer, but there's a reason you're in shackles." Not that I was judging, I had a past filled with my own offenses. My wariness stemmed from deceit and betrayal. I had no way of knowing if he'd help me or slit my throat the first chance he got.

The two luzardees on the wall had reached the roof. It wouldn't take long for them to reach us.

With a growl, the ketaurran stepped backward. "Female, you are outnumbered. Release me now." His deep voice made my insides flutter and warm. The hard set to his jaw said he was a male who expected his commands to be followed.

Too bad I'd never been good at taking orders. "First off, my name's Laria, not female. Second, it's not going to happen." Not until I'd had a long chat with Burke to find out why he'd sent my friends and me after the ketaurran. Thinking about Celeste and Sloane reminded me that they should have found me by now. They might have a problem with punctuality, but they always made an appearance. I hoped the uneasy churning in my gut had nothing to do with their tardiness.

"My apologies, *Laria.* I am Jardun, and you will do well to let me assist you." He raised his shackled wrists again, expecting me to comply.

Irritating male. Since arguing would be pointless and I wanted to save my energy for dealing with the luzardees, I snapped, "Even if I did trust you, I don't have the key, so stay out of my way and let me handle this."

He snorted, then turned to face the male closing in on us from the right. I split my attention between the male scaling toward us on the left and Kowhl. I gripped the blade handle tighter.

"You *will* be coming with usss, and it would be easier if you did not fight," Kowhl said, motioning for the two luzardees to hold their position.

"You will not touch her." Jardun rattled his chains, his growl echoing off the walls. The next few words he spoke were a ketaurran slang dialect, and my translator had difficulty equating them with Earth English. I knew enough of his language to know that it was an insult, that he'd compared Kowhl to animal feces.

Kowhl cringed, taking a step back before gaining his prior composure.

I'd never had much use for overbearing males, but Jardun's fierce protective behavior was refreshing. It spiked the ember of heat building inside me since we met.

"Take them," Kowhl ordered.

Instead of the direct leap I'd anticipated, the luzardee closest to me launched himself over my head, springing off the opposite wall and diving at Jardun. At the same time, the other luzardee landed on the ground and rushed me from the side. The impact knocked me sideways, slamming me into the wall, pain shooting across my shoulder.

He was quick to collar me by the throat, then pin my blade-wielding wrist to the wall's hard surface, the rough sandy finish scraping skin and digging into my arm. As he tightened his grip, the lack of blood flow blurred my vision. Angry that I'd be bruised by morning, and refusing to drift into unconsciousness, I turned and aimed my knee for the luzardee's male parts. I missed him by inches, connecting with the hard muscle on his thigh. It didn't have the crippling effect I'd hoped, but he still groaned and staggered a couple of steps backward.

My blade was mid-swipe when I caught movement in my periphery. The distraction cost me. The aim I'd planned for my opponent's chest missed, grazing his arm, leaving a thin trail of blood on his flesh. He snarled, his gaze darting from his arm to the opposite end of the passageway. "You are outnumbered, female." He smugly sneered as three more luzardees advanced in our direction.

CHAPTER THREE

JARDUN

Luzardees were notorious for their treachery, but they had the resources to obtain the information I'd needed. I knew the risks I'd face when dealing with them, the possibility of betrayal once they'd been paid. It was one of the reasons I had involved Burke. Now those same risks were impacting Laria, and once again, I wondered why Burke chose to put a female in harm's way.

Seeing her retrieve a blade, then handle it as if it were a natural extension of her arm was perplexing. During the war, I had heard whispers about human females skilled with the ability to fight and had shrugged them off as embellished rumors. Was it possible Laria was one of these females and the reason she was associated with Burke? If that was the case, and the stubborn female intended to defend herself against the other males, then she would not be doing it alone.

I glared at Kowhl, angered by his betrayal. It was one thing to come after me, but hearing what he planned to do with Laria was unacceptable and further fueled my rage. I did not want him touching any part of her gorgeous body.

The male would be lucky if he survived to see another day.

Kowhl's shouted command had the other two luzardees springing from the walls. The male hovering near Laria arched through the air. His move was unpredictable, agile, fast. Instead of a direct approach as I'd expected, he bounced off the sandy surface next to me, then landed on my back. The fabric of my coat and the leather vest underneath were no match for the sharp nails he dug into my shoulders. He'd removed his boots before climbing the wall and used the claws on his four toes to anchor himself to my thighs. Ignoring the sharp, pulsing pain and the metallic smell of my blood, I staggered a few steps forward under the impact.

"Laria," I called out, too late to warn her about the luzardee who'd landed on the ground next to her. In order to help her, I needed to dislodge the male clinging to my body. I reached behind me and fought to get a grip. He dodged my grasp, sinking the nails of one hand in deeper as he wrapped an arm around my neck. Whether his intent was to push me into oblivion or end my life, I did not know. Either way I needed to remove the tightness restricting my airway.

The shackles were an annoying hindrance to my fighting abilities, but would not keep me from protecting Laria or myself. I stopped trying to grab him and managed to loop the short length of chain behind his head. Immediately shifting with my back facing the wall, I propelled myself backward. The male's smaller frame was no match for my much larger, more muscular build. The impact forced the air from his lungs. With a painful groan, his grip loosened.

I pushed away from the wall, then jerked my arms to the side, using the chain to pull him off me. Once I had him in front of me, I wrapped the chains around his neck and squeezed.

"Let go." Panic filled his croaky snarl, followed by breathless garbles. He wrenched his body, flipping from side to side like an animal with its head caught in a trap. He clawed at the wide cuffs covering my wrists, the strong metal partially protecting my flesh. I continued to apply pressure until his body slowed to mild jerks, then slumped before me.

I tossed his dead body aside, uncaring that it landed in a heap near the wall. I turned to assist Laria and found her facing off with the luzardee who had attacked her. She handled her knife with ease, brandishing the blade at any attempt he made to get near her. She'd already gotten in several good swipes. Blood trickled down his arm, rage flushing the scales on his cheeks a deep green. If he got his hands on her, I had no doubt he would end her life.

"Jardun, we've got company." She jutted her chin toward the end of the passageway as she continued to protect herself.

I was glad she no longer viewed me as a threat. I was not, however, happy to see the three new luzardees who'd arrived and were taking instructions from Kowhl. They did not remove their boots to access us using the walls. Instead, they approached us in a synchronized manner, their footsteps pounding on the hard walkway. Other than the stun stick Kowhl stood off to the side clutching, the other males were not armed. They had no reason to use a blade, not when their claws made much more effective weapons.

"Move away from the female." I took a threatening step toward the male she held at bay with her blade. He jerked his head toward me, then caught a glimpse of his dead comrade.

His low growl turned into a high-pitched shriek. "You will pay for hisss death."

The distraction was the advantage Laria needed to plunge her blade into the male's side below his ribs. "Not today." She gave him a shove as she pulled out the knife, the blade coated with a thin layer of pale green blood. He gasped and grabbed his side, taking several wobbly steps before collapsing on the ground. The glint of sadness and remorse that passed across her face were quickly replaced with a mask of determination. I understood well that killing was never easy, even if it meant surviving another day.

Overcoming the males, taking their lives if necessary, was the only way Laria and I would be walking out of the passageway alive. She knew it too. It went unspoken in the silent glance that passed between us.

The other three males wasted no time retaliating for their two teammates. Two of them rushed toward me, the other toward Laria.

LARIA

There were times when the conditions on this planet were harsh, and doing unpleasant things to survive was a necessity. I didn't enjoy taking a life, never had, never would. I would've preferred rendering the luzardee unconscious, but they'd made their intentions clear. They'd already betrayed their deal with Burke by coming after us. If they were planning to kill Jardun and turn me into a sex slave, it wasn't going to happen. Not if I could help it.

My gaze locked with Jardun's. There was no judgment in those deep green eyes, only understanding. The connection between us was brief, interrupted by snarls and hisses coming from the three luzardees rushing toward us, prepared to attack.

Two launched themselves at Jardun. The third focused on me. He eyed my knife, then sidestepped, first one direction, then another. He was looking for an opening, a way to get at me without being sliced. I wanted to know how Jardun was faring, but one glance, no matter how quick, would give my opponent the edge he was searching for.

"When we are through with the ketaurran, he will not be able to help you." The luzardee shuffled to my left. "It would be better if you surrender now. I would hate to injure such a well-made body." He flared his nostrils, his beady-eyed gaze roaming over me from top to bottom, lingering on my breasts before returning to my face.

He was purposely provoking me, trying to break my concentration. "Why do I get the feeling you aren't being truthful?" I mirrored his steps, certain he was one of those males who took great pleasure in hurting women.

"Your intelligence rivalsss your beauty, female." His snort turned into a snicker. "I will enjoy avenging my friend'sss death when I spread your legsss."

"And I'll enjoy cutting off a particular body part if you get any closer." My taunt succeeded, and he lunged. I dodged the grab, his claws barely missing my chest. Unfortunately for him, my aim was better, and I left a thin cut on his arm. The need for retribution resounded in his snarl. He was letting his emotions guide his moves, a mistake I planned to use to my advantage. When he spun and grabbed for me again, I held my ground, letting him shove me backward into the wall.

The impact jarred my body, but I ignored the burst of pain along my back and the claws digging into my shoulder and upper arm. I adjusted the angle of my knife and thrust as hard as I could. The sharp tip of the blade easily penetrated his vest and sank into the flesh below.

"Female, you…" His eyes widened, a shocked sheen over the glassy black. He pulled away from me, clutching his midsection. Blood seeped between his clawed fingers, more gurgling from his scaly lips. He'd underestimated my abilities, and it had cost him his life. If he was responsible for enslaving women as I suspected, I wouldn't be losing any sleep over his death.

As soon as he hit the ground, I turned to see what had happened to Jardun and the other two luzardees. Their fight had moved them away from me and taken them toward the other end of the passageway. One luzardee was already lying facedown in the dirt. Whether he was dead or not, I couldn't tell. Jardun was straddling the other. He threw a hard punch, the blow knocking the male into unconsciousness. With a groan, he got to his feet, his gaze immediately landing on me. "Are you all right?"

"Fine, I…" There was movement above Jardun's head. Kowhl, the sneaky male, had waited until we were preoccupied. He was clinging to the wall with one hand and carrying the stun stick with the other. "Behind you!" My warning came too late. Kowhl was already on the ground, jamming the pulse-emitting end of the stick into Jardun's ribs.

"Did you really think I would allow you to kill my crew, then walk away?" Kowhl's eyes flared with a feral savagery. "There are those who will pay well for proof of your death, vryndarr."

Vryndarr? Shocked, I hesitated to react, certain I'd misunderstood what he'd said. There was no way Jardun could be a vryndarr. They were warriors, the drezdarr's elite guard. And if they'd survived the war and still existed, they would never leave their leader's side. Nor would they ever be in a situation where they were shackled and traded for a pouch of coins.

Jardun growled through gritted teeth. He was big, strong, and had barely flinched when he'd been shocked earlier. He should have been able to withstand the jolt, not been forced to the ground. Not unless someone had modified the stick with a lethal setting.

With Jardun on his hands and knees, struggling to get up, he was vulnerable. When he swished his tail trying to defend himself, Kowhl pinned the end to the ground with his boot, further causing Jardun to tense with pain.

Continuing to apply the stick to Jardun's ribs, Kowhl leaned forward and retrieved a short, thin-bladed knife. Apparently, I wasn't the only one who liked to conceal blades in their boots. The muscles in my chest tightened when he raised his arm, poising the blade over the center of Jardun's back.

There was no honor in what Kowhl planned to do to Jardun. Without hesitation, I pulled back my arm and threw my blade. Death would be too easy an end for the traitorous male, so the knife, true to my aim, caught him in the shoulder. I'd learned enough about the luzardee anatomy to know that the blade missed any organs, only penetrated muscle, and wouldn't leave any debilitating damage.

The force caused Kowhl to falter. He shot an unbelieving glare in my direction, then growled a guttural word in his language which translated to a female dog in mine. Not that I cared. I'd been called worse. All that mattered was keeping Jardun alive.

I rushed at Kowhl before he had a chance to recoup and yank out my knife, then propelled him into the wall. I grabbed the stun stick out of his hand and rammed it into his scaly belly, then knocked his knife from his hand. As he doubled over, I withdrew my own blade. His body tensed and jerked, but I continued applying the zapping pressure until he slid down the wall and landed in an unconscious heap. He wouldn't die from his injuries, but he would be in a lot of pain when he woke up.

Jardun had recovered quicker than I'd expected, a lot faster than it would have taken a human male. He seemed a little unsteady, but at least he was on his feet. He blinked several times, then glanced from me to Kowhl. "Female… I mean Laria." He quickly amended when I pursed my lips. "You did this…for me?"

"Yeah, the slimy reptile was going to knife you in the back." I knew it was a cultural thing, but he needed to get over his hang-up about women being able to fight and defend themselves. It hadn't taken me long to discover that the males on this planet also had massive egos, and I didn't want to bruise his by pointing out that I'd just saved his life. I crouched and used Kowhl's pants to clean my knife before returning it to its hidden sheath.

"Are you injured?" He held out his hands as if he were

going to reach for the cut on my cheek, then changed his mind and dropped his arms.

"I'll be feeling the bruises later, but no, I'm fine." His ribs had taken quite a bit of abuse. "And you?"

He rubbed his side, his chains rattling. "I will heal."

"We should go." I kept the stun stick handy in case I encountered any more of Kowhl's crew on our way to find my friends and get out of the city.

He gave me a nod, then fell into step next to me. I gave his profile a quick glance. The male intrigued me. He'd had more than one opportunity to escape during our fight with the luzardees, yet he'd stayed, just as he was staying now. Was it possible he truly was a vryndarr? If so, why was he in shackles? And why had Burke sent my friends and me to retrieve him?

We hadn't gone far when Celeste and Sloane made a miraculous appearance and brought my pondering to a stop. Though the difference in height between my friends was a contrast, Sloane being shorter, with a stunning blue gaze, the confident way they carried themselves was similar. They both had long brown hair pulled back in braids. Celeste's was a few shades lighter and matched the deep cinnamon of her eyes.

"Looks like we missed all the fun," Sloane said as she stepped over one of the downed luzardees.

Celeste used the tip of her boot to turn over the only other luzardee besides Kowhl that hadn't met his demise. "Laria's losing her touch. This one's still breathing."

I was relieved nothing bad had happened to them, but I wasn't over being mad that they were late. "Nice of you two to finally show up. Mind telling me what took you so long?"

"I can honestly say it wasn't my fault this time." Sloane shot Celeste an accusatory glance. "Somebody took her time haggling at the market again."

"Hey." Celeste smacked Sloane's arm with the back of her hand, then pointed at her dark leather, calf-high boots.

"Do you know how hard it is to find someone who makes these boots?" She shoved her hands on her hips. "And is willing to sell them for a decent price?"

Any rant I'd wanted to make dissipated. There was a deeper meaning buried beneath Celeste's defensive behavior. Old memories, old scars, pushed to the surface in my mind. Losing members of our families during the war was the one thing the three of us had in common. Finding a way to help others was how we'd reconnected. We'd lived off the streets, scrounged, fought, and stole to survive. I'd die to protect either one of them and knew they'd do the same for me.

It wasn't what Celeste had purchased, it was understanding why she'd been driven to spend time haggling for a pair of boots she didn't need that concerned me. It meant the nightmares were back. We all had them, but hers were the worst. Sloane and I didn't have any siblings, but Celeste had a younger sister. Or at least she did until Sarus's soldiers attacked the settlement and she'd been forced to watch her die.

There was nothing she could have done, but she'd taken the death hard and blamed herself. It didn't help that she was also twisted in knots over a guy, a ketaurran no less. I didn't know his name, didn't think she'd tell me even if I asked. All I did know was that he'd promised to help get her family somewhere safe, then abandoned her two days before the attack. No one, especially not me, could fault her for using shopping or helping children, any orphan who'd survived the war, as a coping mechanism, a way to feel in control.

"Besides, this is partly your fault." Celeste aimed her glare at me.

I pinched the bridge of my nose, sure I'd missed some critical part of the conversation. "How is you two being late my fault?"

"When we showed up at the bar, you were already gone. The bartender was less than helpful, so it took us a little longer to figure out where you went," Celeste said.

Sloane beamed with excitement. "Did you know he had a blaster?"

"Please tell me you didn't take it." I glared at Sloane, the skilled negotiator, sometimes thief in our group.

Sloane smiled and cracked her knuckles. "It was tempting."

"Until I reminded her about the design flaw in the older models," Celeste said.

Sloane shrugged. "Yeah, not really interested in a weapon that shoots the wrong direction."

"Laria, who are these females?" Jardun had been standing off to the side, listening to our conversation with a skeptical scowl.

"The better question is who's the hottie, and where did you find him?" Sloane interrupted, then sauntered toward Jardun, her gaze rolling over him with admiration.

I didn't find my irritated reaction to her perusal amusing and had to stop myself from stepping between them.

"*Hottie.* Is that a human insult?" Jardun furrowed his brows and looked at me for an answer.

"No, she was complimenting your appearance." I bit back a grin. "To answer your other question, these are my friends, Celeste and Sloane." I pointed at each of them in turn. "And this is Jardun."

Sloane took a step closer to Jardun and touched the chain hanging between his wrists. "Don't tell me this is the package Burke wanted us to retrieve."

"Since when are we doing bounty work for Burke?" Celeste huffed.

"Since never." A deep male voice I'd recognize anywhere echoed off the walls around us.

Celeste, Sloane, and I jerked our heads in Burke's direction at the same time. I was surprised to see him in the city and not back at the settlement. I was even more bewildered to see two more ketaurrans trailing on either side of him.

Burke's dark hair and stubble covering his angled jaw were a contrast to the two males pacing next to him. His height topped six feet, yet he was still shorter in comparison. Both ketaurrans had the same broad-shouldered, muscular build as Jardun. One had dark chestnut hair with cinnamon streaks, a pale blue tint to his skin and scales. The other appeared gruff, intense, almost deadly, with piercing amber eyes and golden hair a few shades darker than his skin. If Jardun really was a vryndarr as Kowhl had said, then I assumed the other two males were probably ones as well.

Burke strolled toward us with a confident, take-charge-of-any-situation swagger.

His arrival triggered an uneasy suspicion that I'd been used as a pawn in a bigger game.

Before I had a chance to ask him what he was doing here, Jardun had moved forward and was glaring at Burke. "Thaddeus, please explain why you did not send me the males I requested."

"Wait." Sloane, always the first to point out the obvious, interrupted by waving her hands. "You're first name is Thaddeus?" She winked at Celeste and me. "How did we not know that?"

"Because it's none of your business." Burke's cheeks reddened, and he curled his fingers into fists. "Sorry, Jardun, I don't recall your request for help specifying males."

I knew Burke had a first name but hadn't given it much thought, but the fact that Jardun knew him on a friendly basis was disconcerting. It furthered my belief that my friends and I were being used in whatever plan, mission, game, the two, or rather four, of them had concocted. Judging by the passive looks on the other two ketaurrans, I was certain they'd been included.

Anger bubbled inside me, the simmering heat bursting along my neck and cheeks. I wanted to know why I'd risked my life battling luzardees for a male who was pretending to be something he wasn't. Determined to get answers, I faced off with Jardun first. "You need to get over your hang-up about females. And you." I shook my head and took a deep breath. "What the draeck, Burke? Why are you here, and who are these guys?" I didn't bother keeping the sarcasm out of my voice.

"More importantly, why did Jardun need rescuing at all?" From the stories I'd heard, the vryndarr were the ones who did the fighting, the rescuing, not the other way around. The tingling dread was back, crawling along my spine like an annoying insect. Instinctively, I knew I wasn't going to like whatever Burke had to say.

Sloane was a little slow to catch on with where my thoughts were going, but Celeste didn't need any prompting. Her trust issues were far worse than mine, and her gaze hadn't left the two ketaurrans since they'd arrived. "Yeah, Burke. Want to tell us what's going on?" She calmly tapped the hilt of her sword and positioned herself on my left.

"Sloane, Celeste, Laria." Burke tipped his chin at each of us in turn. "I would like to introduce Zaedon." He pointed to the chestnut-haired male on his right. "Garyck." He motioned to his left, to the male with the golden hair and amber eyes. "And their leader, Jardun."

I glanced at Kowhl, who was still slumped against the wall, then back at Jardun. "He was telling the truth, wasn't he? You're a vryndarr."

"Yes." A glimmer of guilt flashed in his eyes, then was gone. Jardun cocked his head in Zaedon's direction, holding out his shackled wrists. "Would you mind?"

"Tired of bondage already?" Zaedon grinned. "Even with such beautiful company?" His flirtatious smile was the kind that made women melt.

"Save your humor for later," Jardun growled.

Zaedon chuckled, then slipped a narrow, translucent blade from the hem of his vest. He worked the tip back and forth inside the lock until it clicked, releasing the cuffs. "Better?"

"Much…thank you." Jardun rubbed his wrists, then picked up the shackles where they'd clanked on the ground. With a satisfied smirk, he secured them to Kowhl's wrists.

"So you're a vryndarr, huh?" Sloane, who was easily distracted by curiosity, derailed the direction of the conversation completely by moving closer to Garyck.

The male seemed more than a little scary, and I had no idea why she thought it was a good idea to pester him.

"Are those real?" Sloane was short, her reach stretched when she squeezed the thick, bare muscle of Garyck's forearm.

"I wouldn't do that." Zaedon took a hesitant step toward her, then stopped when Garyck grunted and encircled Sloane's wrist with the end of his tail. "He doesn't like to be touched."

Sloane stopped groping his arm, seemingly more amused than intimidated. "Well, that's too bad." She winked at Garyck, earning her a snort.

My friend's complete disregard for dangerous situations always worried me because it usually got not only her, but Celeste and me into trouble. "Sloane," I warned, then tugged the sleeve of her shirt, encouraging her to leave the grumpy ketaurran alone.

"What?" Her innocent tone spiked my nervousness even more. "He's cute, in a tough, brooding kind of way. Just because he's got all those impressive muscles and doesn't know how to smile doesn't mean I'm afraid of him." Sloane patted his arm one last time, then took a step back.

My friend was quick with her hands, possibly the best thief I'd ever met. If I hadn't seen her in action and known what to look for, I wouldn't have noticed her tuck something shiny into the bag hanging by a thin strap across her chest and resting against her hip.

I elbowed her in the rib. "Give it back."

"Give what back? "She placed her hand protectively over the bag.

I rolled my eyes and smacked her arm with the back of my hand. "You know what."

"I have no idea what you're talking about."

I crossed my arms and glared at her, patiently waiting for her to crack. I ignored the curious stares I was getting from everyone in the group except Celeste.

Sloane rolled her bottom lip into a frustrated pout. "Okay, fine." She reached into the pouch and retrieved a thin silver band inlaid with green and deep blue stones. She turned to Garyck. "I was keeping it, you know, hanging on to it in case it fell off those bulky muscles of yours."

"How did you…" Garyck stared with astonishment at the metal band in her palm, then at his arm where it used to be. I'd bet a week's worth of coins he was wondering how she'd managed to remove the valuable metal without him feeling it.

"One of my many talents." Sloane smirked and slid the band back into place, then ran her fingertip over the gems one last time before giving me a scathing glance. "Happy now?"

"Extremely." Not to mention thankful that no one had said anything about whisking us off to a secluded prison. Maybe it was my imagination, but I could've sworn there was a hint of a smile teasing the ends of Garyck's lips. For a male who didn't like to be touched, he didn't seem to have a problem with Sloane standing so close to him. And what was with the sniffing? Jardun had done the same thing to me shortly after I'd dragged him from the bar.

I directed my attention back to Burke. "Now that we've got the introductions and the touchy-feely part of the program over with, would you like to explain why you went to such extremes to introduce us to your friends?" Unless I was satisfied with his answers, my anger wasn't going to disappear anytime soon.

Jardun glanced at the luzardees on the ground, then at the fading green-and-gold hue in the sky. "It will be dark soon, and no doubt more of Kowhl's males will be searching for them. Perhaps it would be wise to take our discussions indoors."

"We should probably do something with these guys?" Sloane waved her hand at the luzardees.

"She's right. We can't leave them here for someone else to find, especially not the children." There was a sadness in Celeste's eyes.

"We could always dump them in a trash recycler," Sloane said.

"That will not be necessary. We will take care of them," Jardun said.

"Okay." I dragged the word out. "Any suggestion on where you'd like to have this meeting?" I was hoping for someplace public where we could easily walk out if I wasn't happy with what they had to say. The bar wasn't far away, but it would be the first place other luzardees would start looking.

"If you will follow us to our vehicle, we have secured a residence with sleeping quarters near the outskirts of the city," Zaedon said.

Celeste, Sloane, and I had used my transport, a smaller version of a solarveyor, to reach the city. Though it was comfortable and accommodated our needs, including a place to sleep when necessary, it wasn't big enough to carry all of us.

"We have our own vehicle and will follow you." Transportation was hard to come by after the war. It had taken me a long time to find the run-down vehicle I sometimes used as a temporary home. There was no way I was leaving it behind and risk having someone steal it.

Besides, I was still raw about being deceived, especially by Burke, and had no intention of making things easy for any of them. Until I was satisfied I could trust Jardun and the others, I wasn't going anywhere without a means of escape.

JARDUN

There was a time when I would not have worried about staying on the streets of the city after the sunlight had faded from the skies. The war, generated by the old king's brother and his need to obtain the throne, had taken many lives, destroyed many communities, and left many of the planet's inhabitants trying to rebuild their homes. Out of those who had survived, there were some who had embraced a dark path that utilized deadly and greedy means.

I had no idea how many males Kowhl commanded, but the arrival of more luzardees posed a threat I preferred not to deal with. Our upcoming discussion was necessary, and one that should be handled discreetly. It was why I had suggested using the dwelling my friends and I currently occupied.

My thoughts and gaze drifted to Laria. She was unlike any female I had ever encountered. Even though she fought as well as any male, it did not keep me from worrying about her safety or that of her friends. Before Burke's arrival, I had been relieved when the disarray of her hair and the scratch on her cheek were the only outward signs she showed of being in a battle. It had taken every ounce of my willpower to keep from touching her, to convince myself that she remained unharmed.

She did nothing to hide her anger. The color burned brightly on her cheeks. Though she had been deceived and her emotions were warranted, I feared if she was allowed to return to her vehicle, she would leave the city before I got a chance to explain my situation.

"You will not need your transport," I said.

Laria pinned me with a heated gaze. "I don't know who you think you are, but you do not get to tell me what I need and don't need. I'm not leaving my transport behind, and that's final."

I was a vryndarr, a feared warrior, yet her fierce words had me cringing like an inexperienced soldier taking orders from a higher ranking male. I glanced at Burke, silently asking for assistance. I had assumed he was aware that if our teams combined efforts, those working for him would follow my orders without question. I did not know why Laria was being so obstinate about a means of transportation, but I wanted to appease her and would do anything to remove her heated glare.

Burke puffed out an exasperated sigh and stepped in front of Laria. "Come on, be reasonable." He rubbed her arms in a calming manner. "Let's go back to their place and hear what they have to say. We can retrieve your transport in the morning."

I did not understand why I had the overwhelming urge to remove the male's fingers from her skin. Nor did I understand why I was pleased when she shrugged him off, then punched him in the chest below his shoulder with enough force to make him stagger a step backward.

"You know as well as I do that there's a good chance Trixie will be stripped before I get back to her in the morning." Laria clenched her fists as if one wrong comment from Burke would gain him a punch to the jaw.

I thought Laria was upset about her transport and had no idea who this other female was she now mentioned. As if sensing my confusion, Zaedon leaned closer. "I believe the female has given her vehicle a name."

Naming inanimate objects was another human behavior I'd heard about. One I would add to my continually growing list of things I did not understand about the other race.

"If you want me"—she glanced at Celeste and Sloane who each gave her a nod—"us to go with you, to listen to what any of you have to say, then Trixie goes too."

It was apparent that making concessions rather than

arguing was the only way the females were going to cooperate. Before Burke could say anything that would anger Laria further, I moved between them and held up a hand to interrupt. "It is obvious that your vehicle holds great importance to you, so we will accompany you to retrieve it."

"You will?" Laria's tone held a note of suspicion.

I nodded. "Yes."

"Fine." She turned to the other females. "Let's go." She headed toward the opposite end of the passageway without waiting for a reply.

Celeste immediately followed, with Sloane bringing up the rear and stopping long enough to snatch the knife Laria had knocked out of Kowhl's grasp earlier off the ground.

Zaedon crossed his arms and chuckled.

"What do you find so humorous?" I asked, confused by his behavior. If my longtime friend continued to annoy me by staring at Laria's backside, he would soon earn a strike to the jaw.

"It is amusing to watch your interactions with the female. If I did not know better, I would say you liked her."

"She is an excellent fighter with admirable skills." I did not mention how her scent and nearness set my body on fire and made my cock hard. The desire to make her mine grew steadily stronger the longer I was in her presence.

"I do not think it is her skills you are admiring." He smacked the back of my shoulder. "Come, let us go retrieve her Trixie."

CHAPTER FOUR

LARIA

The residence Jardun had taken us to wasn't a quaint out-of-the-way building, and it wasn't someone's home. The exterior showed signs of wear, but nothing like the bar or any of the nearby buildings in that section of the city.

The place resembled a small palace, mostly because it was one. Unlike the settlements where the buildings were constructed using the planet's version of trees, those who lived in the larger cities constructed their homes from stone and sand.

Things had changed so much since the war that I'd forgotten the ketaurran ruler kept residences in several cities. My father was one of many scientists who'd made up the exploration team onboard the *Starward Bounty*. He didn't rank high enough to be included in the meetings the humans had with the drezdarr when we'd first arrived. But I remembered the few visits we'd made to the city and seeing the unique building from a distance.

Upon our arrival, Jardun showed us to our sleeping quarters, which consisted of an elaborate gathering room encircled by separate rooms, each with its own bed. There was even a bathing room containing a large tub with a polished sandstone finish. Now that my body was relaxed, my sore muscles were making themselves known. A fine layer of dirt, sand, and blood covered me. I had every intention of enjoying a long soak later.

"Laria," Jardun waited for me to stop staring at the tub and return my attention to him. "I must leave now. There are matters I need to discuss with Zaedon and Garyck, but I promise to return soon and answer all your questions." His glance included Celeste and Sloane, who'd taken seats on a nearby lounger.

"Okay." There wasn't much else I could say. Arguing would be pointless. Since Jardun had admitted he was a vryndarr, there was a good chance the drezdarr was somewhere inside. Was he the one responsible, the one behind whatever it was that Jardun and Burke had negotiated? Did the matters he planned to discuss with his friends also include their leader? I might have to wait to speak with Jardun, but it didn't mean I couldn't get some answers out of Burke first.

As soon as Jardun left the room and I heard the thud of his boots fade down the corridor, I moved away from the entrance and gave Burke my full attention. "It's time to tell us what's really going on. What kind of deal did you make with the ketaurrans?"

Celeste and Sloane glared at him expectantly. I knew I could count on them to back me up if I didn't get the answers I wanted.

"Laria, sweetheart, it's complicated," Burke said.

I took a step back, pulling away from his placating touch. "Don't you sweetheart me." I wanted to make sure he understood that I meant business. Using a move he'd taught me, I grabbed his wrist and swerved my body, then flipped him over my shoulder. He landed on his back, expelling a whoosh of air. I got some satisfaction knowing I wasn't going to be the only one who'd be stiff and bruised in the morning.

He recovered quickly and got to his feet, making sure to keep some distance between us. "What the hell…" He rubbed his lower back.

"I knew there were times when you kept the truth from me in the past, but I didn't push for all the details because you never put the lives of my friends or me at risk, not without explaining the dangers first. But this—" I slapped my hands on my hips more to keep from walking across the room and using him to vent more of my frustration. "This was downright deceitful and could have gotten me killed."

Burke swept a hand through his short dark strands. "I know, and I'm sorry."

I paced a few steps, staring at the floor and taking in a few calming breaths. "Did you know that Jardun, that they were vryndarr?"

"I did. I've known since the war."

I was certain there was more to the story and was tempted to ask how they'd met. I'd seen Burke's blank gaze before and knew an explanation wouldn't be forthcoming no matter how much I pressed for one. Dredging up the past, especially the years during the war, was painful for all of us. I had no intention of making Burke relive something he hadn't readily wanted to share.

"I still need answers about what happened today. What was going on with the luzardees?" Now that I had time to think about what had transpired, I wondered if the scaly males had been part of some bigger plan. Though I had a feeling the betrayal part hadn't been a consideration.

"Jardun needed our help," Burke said.

"You could've told me…told us." I wasn't letting him get away with a meager explanation, not when I sensed he was still holding back a critical piece of information.

"Or just asked for our help," Sloane said with a shrug.

"I agree. What was the point of putting us in danger?" Celeste asked.

Since I was the one who'd done all the fighting, the one

with the scrapes and bruises, I harrumphed and shot Celeste a *really?* glance.

"You know about their culture. Their women aren't trained for combat, not like I trained each of you." Burke slipped his hands into his pockets. "I didn't think Jardun would believe you were skilled unless he'd witnessed it firsthand."

"Wait a minute." Sloane jumped to her feet, her face beaming as if she'd recently solved an intricate puzzle. "Since the ketaurrans have a thing about protecting women, wouldn't it have been easier to send some of your guys? Why send us?"

"Good point." Celeste pushed off the lounger and moved next to Sloane.

I loved my friends and wanted to hug them for their show of support.

Burke swept his hand through his hair. "You were available and…"

"Do not be overly hard on Burke. He is correct. Had I known he would send females, I never would have allowed it." Jardun's voice washed over me, the deep baritone like a soothing balm to my angered state.

I spun around and stared, my snappy remark never leaving my tongue. Ten of the handsomest human men I knew couldn't compete with the virile male standing in the doorway. He'd removed the long coat, and now a dark vest barely concealed his broad chest. Gossamer scales, a pale green the same shade as the jade in his eyes, covered his breast plate and upper forearms. I was entranced by the way they glistened and longed to run my fingers over their smooth surface.

I forced myself to stop thinking about touching Jardun and focused on what he'd said. "Please tell me we're not back to the females-shouldn't-be-allowed-to-fight thing again." Comments like that weren't helping his cause or scoring him any points. "In case you've forgotten, it was this *female* who saved you from being knifed in the back. I believe I have more than proved that I can take care of myself. Not that it matters, because whatever it is you need, I'm no longer interested."

"Laria, please, just hear what he has to say," Burke said.

In all the years I'd known Burke, I couldn't recall ever hearing him plead a cause. Manipulate and badger until he got what he wanted, yes, but never sound as if he was truly begging. At his core, Burke was one of the good guys, at least most of the time. But he never did anything for free. Ever.

I turned to Burke. "Clearly, the vryndarr are more experienced and capable of handling dangerous situations, so why would they need our help?"

Before he could answer, Jardun stepped between us, giving Burke his back. "Laria, would you take a walk with me? Give me a chance to explain." He held out his hand. "If after hearing what I have to say you choose not to help, I will still compensate everyone for their time."

Greed was never my motivation. Helping those who'd been left with nothing after the war and were merely trying to survive was what gave me the strength to do what I did.

I held no loyalty, nor did I have any use for the ketaurrans or their ruler. Even though I'd never met the old drezdarr, or the new one, for that matter, it wasn't on my need-to-do-before-I-die list. They may have done their best to save the local inhabitants during the war, but they'd done a poor job saving people I cared about. It didn't mean I would intentionally insult him without provocation or refuse to let him explain before turning him down.

JARDUN

I had paused in the corridor long enough to overhear Burke's explanation to the last question Laria and her friends had asked him. He had not been wrong when he'd stated that ketaurran males were protective of females. Our instinct and need to keep them away from all dangers was an inherent part of our nature, stemming from many generations of a warrior-based society. I might not agree with his methods, but he had been wise to send the females, to have Laria provide me with an uninformed demonstration of her fighting skills.

If I had not witnessed the battle with the luzardees firsthand, I never would have believed the beautiful creature standing in front of me was so competently trained.

I held my hand out to Laria, trying to interpret her emotions, and hoping she would not deny me the opportunity to explain. I watched as her angry green gaze slowly transformed to contemplation, then to a reluctant acceptance.

When we'd first arrived at the dwelling, one of several properties owned by the ruling family, I found myself unable to concentrate around Laria. Her scent and my newfound attraction to the female were a distraction. I needed to assess the situation with a clear mind and had excused myself from their room to confer with my trusted friends.

Zaedon, with affirmation from Garyck, had relayed the details of their discussion with Burke prior to meeting us in the city. Burke had stated that the skills Celeste and Sloane possessed equaled Laria's. He was also convinced that their special abilities were far better than those of any of the males under his command. According to Zaedon, Burke had not expounded upon the uniqueness of their talents, so I assumed they were related to the females' fighting capabilities.

The females were the better choice for my mission, but the dangers it posed were risky and life-threatening. When I returned to the set of rooms where they would be residing for the evening, I had every intention of asking Burke to replace them with males for our mission. A resolve that quickly disappeared the instant my gaze met Laria's.

I should have been elated with the knowledge that she had no interest in assisting me with my quest and let her go, not try to convince her to stay. It would have ensured her safety as well as that of her friends. Instead, I was overcome with the desire to keep her close, to prevent her from leaving, and found myself using any means necessary to enlist her help.

"Fair enough. I'll listen to what you have to say." She placed her hand in mine, briefly glancing at her friends before letting me lead her from the room.

My relief was instantaneous, and I kept my hand wrapped around her smaller one until we reached a nearby terrace where we could talk privately.

This building stood taller than the others and provided an uninhibited view of the city. Laria's eyes widened as she glanced at the sporadic lights coming from the surrounding homes and businesses below. She lifted her gaze, taking in the green hue on the two half-moons and the multitude of stars filling the evening sky. "The view from up here is beautiful." She pressed her hands to the smooth rocky edge of the railing, lifting her chin and taking a deep breath of the cool air.

"Yes, it is." I had yet to glance at the panoramic view, too intrigued by the way the light coming from the glow emitters enhanced Laria's features.

She turned to me with a smile, saw the direction of my gaze, and blushed. Embarrassment at compliments was a new side to my female warrior, one I planned to commit to memory, and hoped to utilize again at a later time.

Along with the idea of spending more time with Laria came the thought of her belonging to another. In regard to relationships, the human culture differed from my own. Though she had not mentioned another male's name, it did not mean there wasn't one in her life. Surely if she had a male, he would not allow her to take such risks. Or, at the very least, travel by her side to ensure she remained safe.

These were thoughts I had no right to entertain, yet the need to know was great, so I chose my words carefully. "I mean no insult, but does your male approve of the work you do for Burke?"

For the briefest moment, it appeared as if I had angered her again, then she smiled. "I don't need anyone's approval for what I do. But if there was a male in my life, which there isn't, he would understand." She bit her lower lip, her eyes sparkling with curiosity. "What about you? Doesn't it bother your ketiorra that what you do is dangerous?"

I could not explain why I experienced elation that she knew the ketaurran word for a mate, nor why it made my tail twitch. I longed to wrap it around her shapely legs and pull her closer. "I do not have a ketiorra. Other than the female who birthed me, there is no other in my life."

Her playful smile turned serious, and I was not sure if the news pleased her.

She turned to face me. "Maybe you should tell me what the deal with luzardees was all about and why you need our help."

There were numerous things that had led to the battle earlier today. Some which were confidential and I was not willing to share, at least not yet. "Have you ever heard of a suclorra?"

She shook her head. "No, what is it?"

"It is a rare plant that possesses healing properties."

She appeared perplexed, but remained silent and patiently waited for me to give her more information.

"Someone has found a way to use the blossoms and turn them into a poisonous toxin, one specifically engineered to harm my people." Harm was a mild term. I'd discovered that the toxin was a slow-acting agent that painfully attacked the body and eventually caused death.

She gasped, her gaze widening. "Are you saying that someone created a poison that only kills ketaurrans? How is that possible? To target one species… That's pretty high-tech, and your species, well, I didn't think they were that advanced." Her statement was based on fact; there was no malice or judgment aimed at my people.

"In some things, yes, but in this, no." I sighed at the dire situation and the turmoil that accompanied my discovery. "The information I obtained from Kowhl indicated that a human scientist might be behind the creation."

"My father worked in the labs on the ship with the other scientists who were commissioned to help with the exploration mission." A sadness passed across her face before her gaze turned serious again. "I know the war was Sarus's fault, but I can understand why some humans might be bitter and blame all ketaurrans for what happened. But for someone to design a deadly toxin that could wipe out your entire race…" She shook her head. "It's just wrong."

The humans who had survived the crash on my planet did not ask for the war they had been subjected to several years after their arrival. Many had lost their families during the havoc Sarus had caused. After seeing the additional glint of moisture in her eyes, it was not hard to assume her sire had been one of the casualties. I wanted to pull her into my arms, to console her for the loss, but did not dare.

"That still doesn't explain why you need our help," Laria said.

"The leader of my people has been infected." The guilt-laden burden of failing Khyron weighed heavily on my shoulders.

"I'm so sorry." She placed her hand on my arm. "You have doctors. Can't they create an antidote?"

"It is possible, given time." Time we did not have. "I am afraid the one person who mentored with the humans who possessed the medical experience necessary to develop a cure was taken, along with any of the advancements he had developed." Thinking about the events that could take my friend's life renewed my simmering anger. A ketaurran, someone close to our ruler, was a traitor. A traitor whose identity I had yet to discover.

"I followed the abductor's trail to the luzardees and obtained the information I needed on the physician's location from Kowhl."

"If you got what you needed from Kowhl, how did you end up in shackles?" she asked.

"I believe when Kowhl discovered I was a vryndarr, he decided to take advantage and negotiate a trade for additional coins." It was not one of my better decisions. A decision I had regretted until I realized that meeting Laria had been part of the outcome, and I had learned from Zaedon the importance of the three females to the success of our mission.

"I guess you're lucky Burke has a reputation for dealing with mercenaries and that Kowhl didn't decide to contact somebody else." She turned and pressed her hips against the terrace wall.

I was not sure luck was a factor. By the time Kowhl had betrayed me, I had already sent Zaedon and Garyck to find and retrieve Burke. I had not had an opportunity to discuss what prompted the arrangement with Burke, but I was certain he expected to be compensated well for intervening.

Long moments passed before I found the words I hoped would convince her to help me. "Laria, what is to stop those who created the toxin from developing one that will attack humans as well?" I placed my hand over hers and enjoyed the warmth. "The drezdarr's life is in jeopardy. The future of my people, *and yours*, is at risk. And for that, I need help, and I am willing to pay or do whatever is necessary to obtain it."

She had no reason to trust me, not after what other members of my kind had done to her people. It was a situation Khyron was trying to change. Progress was slow, too slow to aid me now. There were those who operated covertly, who wished to see him fail, evidenced by the poison coursing through his veins. The slow-acting agent was already drying out his scales and, according to Vurell, the physician, would gradually cause all his organs to fail.

"I guess I'm confused." Concern furrowed her brows. At least she had not openly refused, which gave me hope. "Your friends and you are warriors, far better equipped to rescue the doctor. Why would you need our help?"

"I have discovered the location where the physician was taken, but it requires the assistance of humans to extract him. It is my understanding that the other females and you are familiar with the layout of the labs aboard the vessel that brought your people here from Earth."

"Yes, but it was abandoned shortly after we crashed. With the old drezdarr's help, many of the survivors either moved into cities or built agricultural settlements. I'm not sure how that knowledge will help."

"According to what I learned, the wreckage for the vessel that landed in the Quaddrien is no longer abandoned. A mercenary human by the name of Doyle, a male Burke is familiar with, has turned the remains into his personal compound."

"Wait, are you saying that Doyle is the one who kidnapped the doctor?" She wrinkled her nose and pushed away from the wall.

I nodded, waiting for her to finish pondering what I was asking of her friends and her. The wastelands, the name given to the Quaddrien by the humans, was a dangerous, sometimes deadly place. When I originally sought Burke's help, I had considered the dangers we would face, which was why I had wanted the aid of males.

"You need us because we know the layout of the labs." Her chest heaved. "Burke is such an asshole. That explains why he wouldn't give us any information when he sent us to find you. He knew if we found out about Doyle, we'd refuse to do the job." She clenched her fists and muttered as she paced a few steps away from me.

"And you, you could have told me after we'd left the

bar, but you didn't." Her green gaze sparked with a furious intensity. An intensity I would much rather witness during the throes of passion while I thrust into her welcoming depths. Not under the heavy scrutiny of her anger. "You were testing me, weren't you? That's why you offered me coins to release you."

I rubbed the tension building in my neck and focused on the mission, not the thoughts about my personal attraction to Laria. The female was highly intelligent, loyal to her friends, and as fierce as any ketaurran warrior. All qualities that earned merit and my respect.

But my mission came first. The life of my king came first. It should not matter what she thought of me, but for some reason, it mattered a great deal. Her scent, her nearness, made my body burn, made me wish for things I should not desire. "Laria, we live in a time where trusting the wrong person can cost lives. Deceiving you was not my intention, and for that I am sorry."

I reached for a stray lock of hair, then stopped, curling my hand into a fist and dropping it back to my side before I could tuck it behind her ear. "No matter what you believe, I do not wish to see you harmed. If there was any other way to save my friend, I would not ask for your help."

Laria's intense, scrutinizing gaze reached inside me, searching for the truth. "I'll talk to Celeste and Sloane, but I'm not making any promises."

I released the breath I had been holding. No matter how much I wanted to save Khyron, I understood that ordering her to comply would do me no good. And if I were being honest, I wanted, no needed, her to assist me willingly. "That is all I ask."

"Oh, and one more thing." She poked me in the chest, an act a male would never attempt, not if they wished to remain unscathed.

Her lack of fear—of me—both impressed and rekindled my arousal.

"I don't like being lied to. Do it again, and we're done."

"I understand." I confirmed with a nod, then watched the determined sway of her backside as she strode from the room. I wanted nothing more than to follow her, but knew she needed time to speak to the other females without my presence.

CHAPTER FIVE

LARIA

Jardun might not have followed me after our conversation on the terrace, but I'd discovered his trust, like mine, only went so far. Posted in the corridor outside the main door leading to the rooms where my friends and I would be spending the remainder of the evening were two ketaurran guards. They were dressed in matching dark brown vests and pants, the customary dress for the drezdarr's soldiers. They were also armed with impressive swords, the length of the blades extending from their hips past their knees.

I couldn't fault Jardun for being cautious. If our roles were reversed and I wanted to protect the people I cared about, I'd do the exact same thing.

Other than seeing the state of the drezdarr's health for myself, I had no way of knowing if Jardun was telling me the truth. I wasn't sure why I hadn't pressed him for more details. Maybe I was inclined to believe him because of the anguish I'd glimpsed on his face when he spoke about the other male. Or the fact that he was concerned about the future of my people, not just his own.

Then there was the conversation I'd had with Burke. There'd been something in his demeanor as well. I knew there had to be money involved, because Burke rarely did anything without getting paid. I also knew he wasn't one to give his loyalty easily, yet he was willing to risk his life, and ours, to help the ketaurrans. I couldn't pinpoint what had changed my mind, but knew if I didn't do something to help, I'd carry the regret with me forever.

I couldn't deny that I felt a strong attraction to Jardun, but I wasn't going to let my body's reaction to the man influence my decisions. I'd never been one to be careless with my emotions and didn't plan to start now. Unless my usually precise instincts had been affected by his dominating and extremely tantalizing presence, I hadn't gotten any wary vibes from him.

What he was asking of me involved other lives. I might be willing to assist him, but it didn't mean I was ready to trust him or follow him blindly into a dangerous situation.

Convincing my friends that helping the ketaurrans was the right thing to do went beyond difficult. After relaying Jardun's explanation, I stood in the middle of the room waiting for their reaction, which happened a lot quicker than I'd expected.

My friends had been staring at me as if they thought I'd been hit in the head and lost my grasp on reality.

"Laria, you can't be serious." Celeste was the first one to express her opinion and in a voice loud enough to be heard through the closed door leading into the outside corridor. She stiffened her arms, clenched her fists, anger flickering in her cinnamon eyes. "Going after supplies and battling mercs is one thing, but you're asking us to risk our lives to help the ketaurrans. After everything we've been through, the friends and family we've lost, I…" She dropped back onto the lounger, biting back a sob and blinking to keep the moisture from building in her eyes.

The whole conversation might have gone better, been a lot easier if Burke had told us everything from the start. It would have given Celeste time to process the situation. I wanted to believe what Jardun and Burke were asking us to do was for a good cause. It didn't mean I was over being pissed at Burke for deceiving us, and I sure as hell wasn't ready to forgive him yet.

No one could ever say Burke wasn't smart. Sitting in a chair on the opposite side of the room, he knew better than to push the issue with me.

Or maybe his silence was the result of me shooting warning glares in his direction. Either way, he was comfortably seated, long legs stretched out in front of him, wearing a satisfied grin and listening without interjecting any comments.

I wanted my friends to support my decision, but accompanying the ketaurrans had to be their choice. "What if Jardun is right? What if their new drezdarr does care and wants to help our people as well as his own? Can you honestly say you wouldn't do everything you could to make that happen?" I rubbed my forehead against the threatening headache. "Humans weren't the only ones to suffer losses during the war. Sarus's men didn't discriminate when they attacked the cities and human outposts, then killed anyone who got in their way."

I despised the old drezdarr's younger brother, the selfish male who'd started the war and taken so many lives. Sarus might not have wielded the weapons that killed the people my friends and I cared about, but he'd given the orders and was responsible.

Things might have been different if we'd been able to contact Earth after the crash to request a rescue. The ship's entire communication system had been destroyed. Any transmission devices created afterward didn't have the ability to transmit past the atmosphere, leaving us stranded. Building a new home among the planet's inhabitants had been our only choice if we wanted to survive.

The few years prior to the war weren't easy, but they

weren't bad either. I'd been fascinated with the ketaurrans and spent a lot of my time learning about their culture and customs. The majority of the species welcomed us into their communities, and making friends was easy. Only a handful viewed us as unworthy of being on their planet, some striving to make our lives difficult. Others joined forces with Sarus and tried to remove us from existence permanently.

It hadn't been our fight, but we'd been drawn into it nonetheless. I'd seen too many things, too many deaths, things I wish I could forget. It was hard not to blame all ketaurrans for what had happened. After speaking with Jardun, I knew helping them was the right thing to do. I carried enough guilt for the unpleasant things I'd had to do to survive. I didn't want to add the drezdarr's death to the list, not if there was something I could do to prevent it.

If saving the drezdarr's life also meant an eventual end to the hardships and gave my people hope, I was willing to do whatever was necessary to make it happen. But I couldn't do it alone and needed the help of my friends.

Now that it appeared Celeste was over her rant and I'd made my final plea, I glanced at Sloane, trying to gauge her reaction. Her actions were unpredictable, and I wasn't always sure how she'd respond. Of the three of us, she was more easygoing and readily accepted a challenge no matter how dangerous.

She stared at the floor, twirling the end of her brown braid, her nose wrinkled in deep thought. When she finally glanced in my direction, an enthusiastic gleam lit her blue eyes. A gleam which no doubt would eventually lead to trouble.

Sloane settled on the edge of the lounger next to Celeste, then gently squeezed her hand. "Celeste, honey, I know how hard this is for you. But think about the orphans and the others back at the settlement. If saving this guy's life helps make a difference for them, then I agree with Laria. We need to do this—together."

"I…" Celeste turned her head and swiped at a tear before it could trickle down her face. "Fine." She pushed to her feet, smoothing the front of her pants as she stood. "If we do this and I find out afterward they lied to us, or used us for some"—she waved her hand through the air—"nefarious purpose, I'll personally make Jardun and his precious drezdarr pay for it."

Grinning, Sloane got to her feet, then slung her arm over Celeste's shoulders. "And I'll help you." She bobbed her head in my direction, a sign she wanted me to chime in.

"And I'll come along to make sure you two don't get into any trouble or do anything we'll all regret."

I blew out a relieved breath. This was one time I hoped my instincts were right, that Jardun hadn't lied, didn't have a hidden agenda he was keeping from me. I was drawn to him in a way I couldn't explain, and I'd hate to have to make him pay for betraying us.

JARDUN

Shortly after speaking with Burke and learning that Laria and her friends had agreed, if not reluctantly, to assist us, I'd gone to Khyron's quarters to update him on the progress of the plan to rescue Vurell and find a cure. As usual, he was sitting in a chair behind a sandstone desk, reviewing documents.

After listening to me describe the events leading up to and including the encounter Laria and I had had with the luzardees, he said, "Interesting. Burke actually sent females to help you." His grin was filled with curiosity and amusement, not the disbelief I had expected.

"Yes." I nodded.

"And you are sure the females are trained to fight?"

Since I had not witnessed their combat abilities, I did not know the extent of Celeste's and Sloane's skills. I did, however, have a deep appreciation for the precise and graceful way Laria handled a knife. "Burke assures me that all three females possess exceptional skills with a blade, even better than some of the males he commands."

"And what about finding Vurell and the cure?" he asked.

"Burke is confident that with the female's help, he will be able to locate Vurell and the antidote. I have recently learned that her sire was a scientist and she is familiar with the layout of the area we need to access on the ship." Once I was certain the physician was safe and we had the cure for Khyron, I planned to destroy everything in the lab that could be used to create other toxins.

Khyron furrowed his brows. "Are the females aware that entering the Quaddrien is dangerous? Or that Doyle has turned the remains of the human ship into a fortress?"

"They are."

"And yet they are still willing to accompany you. Impressive." Khyron shifted in his seat, his movements slower than they were several days ago. His attempt to disguise his cringing by rubbing his chin did not go unnoticed.

Though he did his best to conceal the extent of his condition by wearing clothes that covered the majority of his body, it pained me to see the dull ash shade to his exposed skin. The intense sparkle in his deep blue eyes had faded. His scales no longer held their vibrant blue luster.

Before Vurell had been abducted, he had concocted a liquid that would temporarily slow down the toxin's effects and hopefully give Khyron more time until an antidote could be developed. Even though the physician had assured me that my friend had weeks, not days, I still feared we were running out of time to save him.

I'd known Khyron since we were younglings. We had fought side by side during the war and would give our life if it meant saving the other. Telling Khyron he should be in bed resting until his health improved or let someone else handle the day-to-day issues that came with his leadership role was moot. He was a proud male and believed that showing weakness of any kind would undermine all he was trying to achieve.

"I assume Zaedon and Garyck will be going with you." Khyron coughed, then leaned back in his chair, clamping his jaw against the pain.

"Yes, we will leave during the first rays in the morning. Thrayn and Raytan will remain behind." I did not voice my concerns about the possibility of another attack on his life, or that I feared his ill health would hinder his ability to protect himself.

The traitor, the person who had infected Khyron, had to be someone who could get close to him. Until I discovered their identity, I would not trust anyone outside my close circle of friends to protect him.

"Then you should see to the needs of our guests," Khyron said, and focused his attention on the documents spread out before him.

"Of course." His dismissal was not meant to be rude, merely my friend's way of preventing me from lecturing him about taking better care of himself. A conversation we had had on several occasions.

Had I not wished to see Laria and thank her personally, I would have ignored his directive and voiced my opinion anyway. Instead, I left him to seek out the female who enticed me in ways I had yet to understand.

CHAPTER SIX

LARIA

I had no complaints about the accommodations Jardun, or I should say the drezdarr, had provided. We weren't permitted to leave our temporary quarters, nor were the guards removed from the outside corridor. The evening meal, a variety of meats and fruits, was good and the bed was comfortable. I'd even enjoyed the bathing tub, lingering long after the water had cooled.

Sleeping in the unfamiliar surroundings hadn't been easy. Because of the occasional work my friends and I did for Burke, the world outside our home in the settlement was filled with dangers. Dangers that could potentially get a person killed. I'd spent too many nights over the last few years in a semi-restful state, my mind always aware of my surroundings.

I'd woken exhausted, a little cranky, and troubled by the concerns I had about traveling into the wastelands. To say I was more than a little worried about what we'd face once we entered an area most of the planet's inhabitants avoided would be an understatement. Knowing we'd be traveling with three lethal vryndarrs who'd survived far worse situations eased some of my stress.

While the solarveyor, a much larger and more accommodating transport powered by the sun's rays, was being loaded with supplies, Jardun provided us with additional information about the route we'd be taking to our destination. Our first stop would be an outlying outpost near the border of the Quaddrien manned by a handful of the drezdarr's soldiers.

Out of all the human members of our group, Burke was the only one who'd returned to the wastelands shortly after the crash. He'd been in charge of a small team sent to retrieve whatever could be salvaged and used to build our new lives. According to him, anything salvageable on the levels they could access had been stripped and removed. It was the reason I was surprised when I heard Doyle and his band of mercs had occupied the wreckage. As far as I knew, the ship had landed in an area far from any food and water sources. Why the male had chosen that location baffled me.

Human technology was more advanced than ketaurran. The surviving scientists found it difficult to replicate the modernized devices used on the ship with the planet's resources. After Jardun told me about the toxin, I wondered if there were other technological items that had survived the crash that Doyle and his men had managed to find.

I imagined all the horrible things that could happen to the inhabitants if someone like Sarus, someone possessed with the need for power, decided to use what they found to start another war, and shuddered.

The trip would take most of the day, and I planned to spend part of it relaxing, trying to recuperate from the beating I'd taken the day before. Once we were underway, I'd moved farther back in the vehicle and curled up on a bench-like seat and stared outside one of the portal panes. Not that I could see much of the landscape through the heavy sheets of water pummeling the ground. The storm had started shortly after our departure and showed no signs of stopping. The horizon was one long strip of varying shades of gray, the buildings in the distance tiny dark blobs.

The others remained near the front of the transport. Garyck was in charge of operating the vehicle and concentrated on the controls. Zaedon was busy entertaining my friends with stories of his exploits and heroism. The bits of conversation I hadn't tuned out sounded as if he'd done some embellishing and elicited rounds of laughter. I'd even heard an occasional giggle coming from Celeste.

Thinking about all the what-ifs involved with this trip hadn't helped the persistent throbbing from the headache I'd developed the night before. I closed my eyes and leaned forward to massage my neck.

"Laria." At Jardun's deep voice, I opened my eyes and dropped my hands to my lap. Why out of all the males I'd met on the planet did this one have such a warming effect on my system?

He sat down opposite me, his bulky frame taking up most of the seat. "This will help." He held out a drinking receptacle containing a steaming yellow liquid.

The weather had slowed us down, and though he offered me a warm smile, I could tell by his solemn demeanor that the delay wore heavily on him. The longer it took us to obtain the antidote, the greater the risk to the drezdarr's life.

"What is it?" I sniffed, then wrinkled my nose at the bitter aroma.

"It is called creevea and has a natural stimulant that will assist with your weary condition."

My quarters didn't have anything resembling a mirror or reflective surface, so I had no way to check my appearance before we left. "Do I look that bad?"

He quirked a brow, the hint of a grin on his lips. "You are remarkably beautiful."

Had he thought I was looking for a compliment with my question? My cheeks heated, and I held back an embarrassed groan.

"You appeared to be experiencing pain, and the creevea will help." He leaned forward and gently touched my temple. "I believe it is similar to one of your human drinks. I remember reading something about it in the history data books the leaders from your ship had given our people shortly after your arrival. I believe you refer to is as cuffy."

I giggled. "Coffee. It was called coffee." And the supplies of the favored beverage saved from the ship had been depleted long ago. If there was any left on the planet, whoever had it was doing a great job of keeping it hidden.

"Coffee." He repeated the word. "Sometimes it is difficult to translate the pronunciation accurately. Please continue to correct me if I do not speak your language properly."

I was impressed he'd taken the time to learn more about human habits and interests. Even more so that he'd attempted to say it in my language and not his. Not that it mattered—I had a universal translator surgically implanted via a tiny needle under the skin near my right ear. It was one of the few technological advances that the scientists back on Earth had the foresight to develop.

Everyone who'd participated in the colonist exploration program, including all family members, were provided with a device. This planet hadn't been our original destination, but now we were here, it had sure made communication and the process of integration into our new and permanent home a lot easier.

"You speak my language very well. I have no complaints." Complimenting and flirting, something I hadn't engaged in for such a long time, came easily with him. Maybe too easily.

There were times when I wondered what life would have been like, how differently things would have turned out, if Sarus hadn't started the revolt that took so many lives. Things were different now. Life was hard, and what I did to survive was dangerous. I couldn't afford to allow my emotions or my growing attraction to Jardun to get in the way of the mission.

We might live on the same planet, but we came from different worlds. Even if we survived and were successful, after we returned to the city I'd never see him again. He'd go back to doing whatever the vryndarr did and I would return to the settlement, continue working with Burke.

"Are you not going to try it?" He'd noticed that I still hadn't taken a drink. "I promise it is safe and will not harm you in any way."

After our conversation the evening before, he must have realized that building trust between us was going to take some time. His reassuring smile put me at ease, and I dared to take a sip. Surprisingly, the liquid tasted better than it smelled, so I swallowed some more. "Not bad."

"But not good either." He grinned, though his gaze seemed more focused on me than the drink.

I took another sip. "Thank you, I'm starting to feel a lot better." Besides my disappearing lethargy, the pounding in my head was subsiding. Even my muscles weren't as sore as they were earlier.

I thought the heat radiating through my body had less to do with the drink and more to do with his nearness and having his long leg pressed against mine.

JARDUN

As much as I enjoyed spending time with Laria, getting close to the female was not something I could afford to do. After supplying her with the creevea to help her bodily aches, I'd returned to the control area to monitor our progress for the remainder of the trip.

The storm had abated somewhat by the time we reached our destination. It did not, however, prevent our group from getting drenched after leaving the vehicle. On the way to the larger of three buildings, we passed another solarveyor similar to ours. Sitting next to it was a much smaller transport designed to carry two or three passengers.

Prior to the war, and because of its strategic location, Sarus had taken up residence on the far side of the Quaddrien. After several of the scattered farming communities closest to the mountainous perimeter surrounding the wastelands had been attacked, the remainder were abandoned. Khyron's father had converted them into military outposts and manned them with a handful of soldiers.

A direct approach across the wasteland's flat sandy terrain could be easily spotted by Doyle and his men, making it more difficult to extract Vurell and the antidote. Therefore, Zaedon, Garyck, and I had chosen an alternate route, one that would conceal our presence. I had chosen an outpost closest to one of the few places where a transport could enter the wastelands.

The structure was the only one with light peeking out around the edges of several partially concealed windows. Because the occasional storm had a tendency to drop large amounts of water and cause flooding, the floor of the building was a foot off the ground and supported by thick braces. A wide platform similar to a covered porch extended along the front of the dwelling.

"This sand is worse than the stuff back home," Celeste whined, then stomped her boots, leaving a trail of reddish-gold clumps on the covered platform.

Zaedon chuckled and stepped onto the platform behind her. "Do not worry, zyrdena, the mud will fall off easily once it dries." The teasing words that translated into little princess in our language seemed appropriate for the female who was overly concerned about her footwear.

"Sure it will." Celeste rolled her eyes and stamped her feet a few more times.

Uneasiness washed over me as I waited for the remainder of the group to join me before approaching the entrance to the building. I glanced at the surrounding area and didn't see any movement, nothing suspicious. "I find it strange that the rumble of our vehicle's engine has not drawn the attention of those inside." I directed my comment to Garyck and Zaedon, knowing they would use caution and ensure the females remained behind me and safe.

After receiving a brief nod from both males, I gave the door a hard rap, then pushed it open. As soon as I stepped inside, a ketaurran male growled, "Who the draeck are you? And what are you doing here?"

He'd been sitting at a rectangular table in the center of the room and immediately shot to his feet, knocking his chair backward in the process. The disregard he held for his position was apparent in the way he was dressed. His feet and chest were bare, the dark pants of his uniform rumpled. The sword that should have been attached to a leather belt at his waist was nowhere to be seen.

The human male on his left barely flinched. Dressed in drab tan pants, he remained seated with his long legs crossed at the ankles and propped on the end of the table. His light brown hair brushed his nape, and his prominent jaw was clean-shaven. His gaze remained alert and wary as he inched his hand under the table, no doubt fingering a weapon hidden from view on his hip.

"My name is Jardun, and we are in need of a place to stay for the evening," I said as I scanned the rest of the room. Other than a few pieces of furniture, the area had been stripped of any personal items that would enhance its dull appearance. It was also in need of some cleaning. A thin layer of dirt coated the floor, and a stench filled the air. Several platters covered with food crumbs sat haphazardly on one end of the table.

The sound of hasty footsteps preceded two more soldiers before they entered the room from a corridor on the opposite wall. It appeared as if the males had taken the time to cover their feet with boots. Otherwise, their appearance was no better than the male glaring at us.

I pursed my lips in disgust. These males were a disgrace and lacked the discipline of true ketaurran soldiers. Judging by the flicker in Zaedon's dark turquoise gaze and Garyck's grunt, their assessment of the males closely matched mine.

The vryndarr did not wear uniforms or articles of clothing that advertised our existence. I had no idea what we would encounter during our trip, nor did I want Doyle or his men alerted to our presence. Following Khyron's suggestion, we had traveled under the guise of a soldiering unit ordered to make random inspections at the outposts along the Quaddrien. It was why Zaedon, Garyck, and I had dressed in military attire prior to making the trip. We also had a fabricated story about Burke and the females being stranded in case anyone asked why they were traveling with us.

To make the tale believable and because the females' long blades would draw attention, they had agreed to leave their swords in the transport. I did not stop them from hiding a blade or two within their clothing.

"This is an outpost, not a boardinghouse." The male with bare feet stomped around the table to stand with the new arrivals.

I stripped out of my long hooded coat, allowing them to see my vest, which designated a rank high enough to intimidate. One soldier gasped; the other widened his eyes.

"I will relay your response to the drezdarr. I am certain he will be pleased by your attentiveness to your positions." I took my time glaring at the face of each male in turn, ending with the human, who remained seated.

The human studied us through a narrowed gaze, giving the females an appreciative glance before letting his focus linger on Burke. He dropped his feet to the floor with a loud thump, then grabbed a mug from the table and drained whatever liquid was inside. "Tarzel, I think I'll head out and let you see to your guests." After slipping on the coat draped over the back of a nearby chair, he gave me a brief nod as he stepped around me on his way out of the building.

It was obvious the human was on friendly terms with the soldiers, which made me wonder what he was doing at the outpost. The location was isolated, too far from any cities, not worth a trip without a purpose. Being this close to the wastelands, there was always the possibility he was involved with or worked for Doyle. If I was correct about the latter, preventing the human from leaving and asking him questions could jeopardize our mission.

I decided it would be better to question one of the other males, preferably the one in charge, about any recent activities. "Which one of you is in command?"

"I am the leader here." Tarzel, the male the human had addressed before his departure, was the tallest of the three males and also the one wearing the least amount of clothing. "There are additional beds in the back of the building that you can use. I will have one of my males accompany you while I show the pleasure females to our rooms."

The other two males were openly stared at Laria, Celeste, and Sloane. The way they puffed out their chests and leered had my tail twitching. Their lack of surprise at the females' presence made me wonder if this wasn't the first time human females had visited the outpost.

During the war, I'd heard rumors of females being stolen, sometimes bartered or sold as slaves to be used for sexual pleasure. There had been a recent whisper or two that it might still be happening.

The idea that the males of my own kind would participate in such a horrible act disgusted me now the same as it had then. Once we returned to Aztrashar and Khyron's health was repaired, I planned to have a lengthy discussion with him about the situation and investigate it further.

Tarzel moved closer to Laria, grazing her arm with his fingertips. "Come with me, female. You can share my bed for the evening."

My rational mind knew Laria was more than capable of handling Tarzel's advances. But all logical reason escaped me the instant his hand circled her wrist.

"Hey, get your…" was all I heard her say before I snarled and yanked him away from her. After shoving him against the nearest wall, I collared him by the throat. "Do not touch her. Ever."

Tarzel made a strangled noise and clawed at my wrist. His tail slapped against my leg and thumped against the wall.

I squeezed a little tighter. "Am I clear?"

Since my actions barely allowed him to breathe, his acknowledgment came out garbled. After I released Tarzel and shoved him toward the other males, I noticed that Garyck and Zaedon had taken protective positions on either side of the females. They had their hands inches from reaching for the blades at their hips. Burke stood off to one side, wearing an amused grin, yet maintaining a wary stance.

"The females are under our protection and will be accompanying us when we leave in the morning. They are off-limits and will be provided with private sleeping quarters." Zaedon and Garyck had also removed their coats and were reinforcing my words with scrutinizing glares of their own. "Are we understood?"

One of the lower-ranking males kept his gaze trained on the floor. The other bobbed his head. Tarzel pinned me with an angry glare and rubbed his neck. "Understood." Disdain edged his cracked voice.

A few seconds later, the door burst open and a fourth, much younger male came rushing into the room. Water dripped from his dark hair, the strands plastered to his face. "I finished walking the perimeter and heard a transport." He tugged at the loose-fitting pants of his uniform. The males in my group went completely unnoticed as soon as he saw Celeste. "They brought more females." His voice turned breathy, and lust filled his gaze.

Had my suspicions been correct? Were the males expecting someone else, someone who would be supplying them with females?

"Be quiet, fool." The male standing closest to the young one warned through gritted teeth. He elbowed him in the ribs, then tipped his chin in my direction.

It was easy to determine the instant the young male noticed the dark green shade of my vest and realized the rank of my uniform. His excitement instantly faded to fear. He respectfully bowed his head, then moved backward and closer to the others.

The vryndarr did not have ranks, nor did we follow the protocols of a soldier. We were elite warriors, our main purpose to serve and protect the drezdarr. My friends and I had done many unpleasant yet necessary things. Things we would gladly do again if it meant giving all the inhabitants on our planet a chance to survive. Some of our directives, the roles we were required to perform, had changed as a result of the war. I was glad that our current performance appeared to be working.

"Are there any other males under your command, anyone else outside?" The question was one that would be asked during a regular inspection. Knowing the exact number of males we'd be dealing with was important information to have if things didn't go the way I'd planned.

"No, this is everyone," Tarzel said.

"What are the other two buildings used for?" I wanted a secure place where the females would be safe and away from the scrutiny of the soldiers. It would also provide us with privacy to discuss our plans for infiltrating Doyle's compound.

"Everything here was left over from the humans who

farmed the settlement before the war. The other two buildings are similar to this one, only smaller." Tarzel ran his hand through his hair. "Occasionally, humans traveling to the city will pass through here. We let them use the building on the right because it contains multiple sleeping quarters. The other is used to store additional supplies."

The lands surrounding the Quaddrien were not safe. I did not believe humans with families would travel through this area. Mercenaries or those who'd been loyal to Sarus and wanted to avoid capture were more likely the visitors he was referring to.

"Can we assume the male who left was one of these travelers?" Zaedon seemed to have reached the same conclusion.

"You mean Rick? He stops here on his way back and forth to the city." The young male's helpful answer gained him a low snarl from Tarzel.

I was about to ask where Rick had been coming from when Burke interrupted. "Why don't we head over to the other building? It's been a long day, and I'm sure the women would like to get settled."

I got the impression Burke had something important he wanted to share but did not want the other males to overhear the conversation. "I agree."

"But there's not much over there." The young one was staring longingly at Celeste again. "She, I mean they, might be more comfortable…"

I cut him off. "I am certain the quarters will fulfill our requirements. If we need anything else, we will let you know." It was obvious the outpost lacked some of the luxuries found in the city, but as long as we had food and a place to sleep, I wasn't worried.

Burke and Garyck left the building first, with Laria, Sloane, and Celeste falling in behind them. I knew Zaedon remained by my side in case any of the males were foolish enough to try anything.

Once we reached the safety of the other building,

Garyck and Burke returned to our solarveyor. They moved it closer to the structure before retrieving the bags containing the additional blades, clothing, and supplies we had acquired for the trip.

Zaedon appeared at my side shortly after Laria and her friends left the main room in search of sleeping quarters. "You are once again contemplating your theory that Sarus is still alive, aren't you?" He lowered his voice so we would not be overheard in case the females returned.

It was a topic Zaedon and I had discussed several times. Sarus's body had never been found. Since the war had ended, my friends and I had encountered those who were still loyal to the male on more than one occasion. The attack on Khyron's life and Vurell's kidnapping were too well planned. Sarus was the only one who would gain anything from his death. "Perhaps." I crossed my arms. "I am more concerned with the possibility of females being furnished to the outposts."

"We both know Khyron would never allow his soldiers to be supplied with females, willing or otherwise."

"I agree and believe he is unaware of the situation." Khyron, like the rest of us, was a man of honor. He would protect any and all females with his life.

"Do you think this has anything to do with the rumors we have been hearing about the disappearing human females?" Zaedon asked.

"I do not know." It was bad enough dealing with mercenaries and their treacherous ways, then wondering if any of the soldiers were involved. It would be even worse to discover that someone was abducting human females and forcing them to be sex slaves.

"If you plan to investigate when this mission is over, I wish to be included," Garyck said from the open doorway as he carried more supply bags into the room. He dropped the bags on the floor, then returned to the platform outside.

"I assume you wish to be included as well?" I spoke to

Zaedon, then glanced over my shoulder at Garyck, who was closing the door behind him.

"Me, miss an opportunity to rescue young damsels? Never." Zaedon laughed.

"Damsels, huh?" Burke smirked at my friend's use of the human term.

"Anyone hungry?" Garyck held up the carcass of a small reptilian animal he'd taken the time to hunt for our evening meal.

"Come on." I clapped Zaedon on the shoulder. "We can discuss what a bad decision it was to let you read the Earthers' history data later."

CHAPTER SEVEN

LARIA

Shortly after Garyck retrieved our belongings from the solarveyor, Celeste, Sloane, and I set off to find a place to sleep for the night. There were several darkened rooms at the end of a short hallway. I chose the one to my right, then felt along the wall inside until I found the switch for the glow emitter. After giving it a single tap, the interior filled with light. "At least they kept the solars charged."

It was obvious the males manning the outpost hadn't expended any energy maintaining the buildings. A thin film of fine-grained sand coated the floor, and a stale smell lingered in the air. The inside of the building may have lacked a recent cleaning, but the furniture and bedding appeared to be in decent condition. The room contained four separate beds, each designed to accommodate one person. Two of them were shorter in length than the others.

Finding the varying sizes wasn't uncommon. Nor was having more than one family live and work together on the small farming settlements. I walked over to the bed closest to the door, then set the bag containing my belongings on the floor.

"Looks like whoever lived here before had several young children." Celeste skimmed her fingertips along the shortened bed mat as she moved across the room.

"We can check out one of the other rooms." I was afraid being reminded of children made Celeste think about the sister she'd lost.

"No, this is fine." There was a tightness in her voice that I wished I hadn't heard. "Besides, there's no way the guys will fit in these beds." She glanced at me over her shoulder, a half smile on her lips.

Sloane giggled and wandered toward one of the smaller beds. "Yeah, can you imagine one of the ketaurrans trying to squeeze their big hulking frames onto one of these?"

Thinking about a bed, any bed, and Jardun at the same time had heat rising on my cheeks. I quickly pushed the thoughts aside and removed the blanket from my bed. I gave it a thorough shake to make sure no little crawly things had made a home in it. I especially hated the crognats.

The pale gold creatures were a cross between a beetle and a miniature lizard. They liked to find dark, cool places to hide. Most of the time, they were harmless unless you happened to roll over on one in your sleep. That's when you discovered they had a sharp stinger and knew how to use it. They might not be poisonous, but the nasty red welt from their sting burned for a couple of days.

After doing the same with her blanket, Sloane knelt in the middle of the bed she'd selected beneath the room's only window. She pushed aside the two sheets of faded and worn fabric used to keep out sunlight, then stretched out the accordion-style interior shutters that formed a protective panel across the panes. After securing the pin-type locks in place, she reached behind her back and retrieved the two thin knives she'd hidden inside her boots.

"What are you planning to do with those?" Celeste

asked.

Sloane jammed one blade on each side of the frame between the wall and the shutter. "It's an extra precaution in case the creepy guys next door get any ideas." She spun around and plopped on the edge of the bed, then flashed Celeste and me a mischievous grin.

Using the knives as reinforcement was a deterrent. They wouldn't prevent someone determined to get inside from entering, but they would rattle against the pane and provide us with a warning. As an additional precaution, I planned to sleep with one of my blades tucked under the bed's padding.

"Definitely a good idea." I shuddered, remembering what Tarzel had planned for us. Prior to our arrival, we'd agreed to let Jardun and the other males perform their imaginary roles as the drezdarr's high-ranking emissaries. After seeing the so-called soldiers and their human friend Rick, my warning senses were tingling that there was something extremely wrong with the situation. I was glad I'd tucked a thin blade inside my boot for protection, and was even happier when Jardun announced we'd be spending the night in a separate building.

The great thing about having friends who'd shared the same life experiences and fought by your side through some incredibly high-risk situations was the ability to communicate to one another without saying a word.

Celeste, Sloane, and I had shared one of those knowing looks the minute we'd entered the main outpost. It was a silent and unanimous decision to forgo Jardun's instructions if things headed in a bad direction.

Celeste plopped down on her bed, then patted the thinly padded surface. "Not much to it, but I guess it beats sleeping on one of the benches in the transport."

"So, Laria." Sloane drew out my name as if it were a question. She was swinging her legs up and down like an excited child.

"Yeah," I replied, then leaned against the wall with my

arms crossed, waiting to see what kind of trouble she planned on starting.

"Did you notice the way Jardun's muscles rippled when he pinned Tarzel to the wall?"

Yes, I'd noticed. It was hard not to. The male had a presence that demanded attention. I didn't think there was a female on the planet who wouldn't stop to notice him.

"And the growling…quite an impressive display." Celeste pushed off her bed, then walked over and plopped down next to Sloane. "I think he has a thing for Laria."

Playful teasing or not, this wasn't a discussion I wanted to have with my friends, yet a part of me was curious to hear what they had to say. "And why would you think that?"

"Oh, I don't know. Maybe because he was going to rip the guy's throat out for touching you," Sloane said.

"Do I need to remind you that the ketaurrans are hardwired to be overly protective of women?" It was the same excuse I'd been telling myself since the incident with the other males.

"Oh, I'd say he's hardwired, all right. Or at least he gets har…"

Celeste nudged Sloane with her shoulder, cutting her off before she could finish. "Is sex all you think about?"

"Nooo. Sex is *not* all I think about." Sloane smirked and returned the nudge. "Although, you have to admit, with all those firm bodies running around, there's a lot of temptation."

I'd seen the way she watched Garyck, and I couldn't resist getting in some teasing of my own. Anything to keep her focus off Jardun. "Are you sure it's not one particular muscled male whose body you can't keep your eyes off of?"

"No clue what you're talking about," Sloane huffed, then further added to her denial. "He's too grumpy for my tastes."

"Uh-huh." Celeste winked at me.

Burke appeared in the doorway and leaned against the frame. "Everything okay in here?"

"Fine, why?" Celeste's humor faded with the cool look she shot in his direction.

We were all still disappointed by the way he'd deceived us, but Celeste was known to hold a grudge way longer than Sloane and I.

"Come on, I said I was sorry." He held out his hands and took a few steps into the room. "If I promise not to do it again, would you at least pretend to forgive me?"

It was hard to resist his charming grin, and hearing him use the word "promise" was an added bonus. Burke was smart. He knew if he wanted to continue getting our help in the future, he'd have to stand by his word.

"What do you think?" I glanced at Sloane, then Celeste.

Sloane shrugged. "I guess I can pretend."

Celeste tapped her chin, then, after a long pause, finally said, "I suppose…for now."

Yeah, she was definitely holding a grudge. One I was certain she'd passively make Burke pay for during the entire trip.

"Great." Burke clapped his hands together. "So who's hungry?"

JARDUN

"I'm telling you, the heat is too high. You're going to burn the meat," Sloane said as she tried to reach past Garyck and adjust the solar regulator on the countertop cooking unit.

Garyck snorted and swatted at her with his tail. Sloane stepped back, frowning. "Do that again and I'm going to tie the end in a knot."

Listening to the two argue as they prepared our meal was most amusing. The small female's chatter was focused on critiquing Garyck's cooking abilities. There was a time, before he was captured and tortured by some of Sarus's men, that my friend laughed and engaged in any discussion. Now he only spoke when he had something relevant to say. The conversation between the two was mainly one-sided, but Sloane did not seem to have any problems interpreting Garyck's grunts accurately.

Celeste and Laria were standing nearby, leaning against another section of the counter and sipping drinks. I was not sure if they were there to protect their friend from Garyck—he would never harm a female—or were enjoying the couple's banter. Their occasional giggle made me believe they found the interaction as entertaining as I did.

Laria glanced in my direction, caught me staring, our gazes locked briefly before she returned to silently observing Sloane torment Garyck. She fascinated me, and not for the first time since we'd left the city had I questioned my decision to allow the females to accompany us. I knew she was well trained; I'd witnessed her skills firsthand. And, according to Burke, Celeste and Sloane were equally equipped to handle whatever we faced.

I leaned back in my chair and took a long, much-needed swallow of the fermented ale Zaedon had found when he inspected the items kept in the adjacent building used for storage. I relished the burn as the bitter homemade brew trailed down my throat.

I contemplated the delays in our progress to find Vurell, worried whether or not he was still alive and if we would be successful in obtaining the antidote for Khyron.

It seemed even the weather had aligned with those determined to keep me from saving my friend. The storm had passed, but the substantial amount of water that had fallen prevented us from leaving before the rise of tomorrow's sun. The long trip combined with the overcast sky had depleted most of the solarveyor's energy reserve. It would only take a few hours of direct sunlight to replenish, but it was time we could not afford to spare.

The success or failure of this mission rested on my

shoulders, on my leadership, on my abilities to keep my team and the others safe.

My thoughts drifted to the males in the other building and the possible threat they posed. Most ketaurran soldiers did well in a fight, but their skills were no match for a vryndarr. Besides our expertise with a blade, we were trained to be adept at stealth and able to move through the shadows undetected. I had learned long ago to improvise, to use anything in my surroundings to survive.

As I replayed my interaction with Tarzel, the image of his hand wrapping around Laria's wrist filled my mind. I had scented his arousal, knew that he wanted her badly. My body tensed, and I was forced to suppress a growl to keep the others from questioning my thoughts.

I did not trust any of the males and believed the females would not be safe until we were far away from the outpost. In case my suspicions were correct, Zaedon, Garyck, and I would take turns patrolling the surrounding area throughout the night.

"Food smells good." Zaedon strolled into the room from the corridor leading to the sleeping quarters. One of the rooms provided a view of the building occupied by Tarzel and his males. "Their lights remain on, and no one has exited the dwelling," he reported before pulling out a chair and sitting.

Burke picked up an empty mug from the table and filled it with ale before taking the seat next to mine. "We may have another problem."

"If you are going to warn me about the other males, it is not necessary," I said.

"No, this has to do with their friend Rick." He placed his drink on the table, absently running his fingertips along the mug's exterior.

I had hoped the issue regarding Laria and her friends was the only thing I needed to worry about before we left in the morning. I rubbed my forehead, the tension I'd eased earlier returning, and waited for Burke to continue.

"He looked familiar." Burke scratched the dark stubble on his chin. "I know I've seen him before, but I can't remember where."

"I got the impression he recognized you too." Celeste placed a stack of empty plates on the end of the table, then set one in front of each seat.

"Do you think he's one of Doyle's men?" Laria asked as she helped Sloane carry the platters of meat and set them in the middle of the table.

"Being this close to the wastelands and not believing in coincidences… I'd have to say it's possible," Burke said.

I had worried that Rick might somehow be connected to Doyle as well, that word of our arrival would reach the mercenary long before we left in the morning. If Burke's speculations were correct, then Doyle would be prepared for our arrival and be monitoring the main access road leading into the Quaddrien.

I waited for everyone to take a seat and finish putting food on their plates. "What more can you tell us about Doyle?"

"He's a mean son of a bitch. Cruel to his men…obsessed with power." Burke speared a piece of meat with a thin blade and held it inches from his mouth. "I hated being under his command when we were on the ship." He took a bite, chewed, swallowed, then continued. "After the crash, he got worse. It was like something snapped inside his mind, and he turned on anyone who voiced an opinion different from his."

Burke glanced reflectively around the table. "Some of the guys who worked under him before we arrived stayed with him. The others ended up following me to the settlements. After he took up with Sarus, we were afraid of what he'd do to the families, so we stayed together, did our best to protect them."

This was the first time Burke had offered an explanation of why he did what he did. I had never encountered Doyle personally but knew the two males were very different. Doyle was a heartless mercenary driven by power and greed. Lives, unless they gained him coins, held no value.

Burke at least possessed some ethical standards. His standards did not always reach a high level, but they did exist. And there were times, though rare, when his aid and acquisition talents did not come with a price.

"His men are ruthless, so everyone needs to be extra careful once we get inside the ship." Burke's gaze moved from Celeste to Sloane, then to Laria, where it remained the longest.

I was annoyed by the extra attention the male was giving Laria and quickly changed the subject. "Doyle and his men are not the only things we need to worry about. There are creatures in the Quaddrien who do not like visitors." I lifted the last piece of meat on my plate to my lips.

Sloane pushed her plate aside. "Please tell me we aren't going to run into any more of those desert dwellers."

"You mean the luzardees?" I asked.

Sloane snapped her fingers. "Yes, them."

I understood her concern. A handful of the males could be easily dealt with, but greater numbers would put us at a very bad disadvantage. "Even though they make their homes in desert areas, they prefer to stay away from the wastelands."

"So, what kind of creatures are you talking about, then?" Worry crept into Celeste's voice.

"The kind that slither and do not hesitate to attack if you get too close to their nest." Zaedon grinned, then reached for the last of his ale.

My friend's reference to the snakkrils was accurate. The creature avoided the heat and hunted during the evening, burrowed deep in the sandy areas, keeping their nests where it was cooler. If the rains had flooded the area, the top layer of sand could have shifted locations, distorting the solid areas. If we were not careful, we could inadvertently travel across a nest and awaken one of the nocturnal animals.

I knew from experience how difficult it was to survive in the Quaddrien. As a young male barely able to wield a practice sword, I'd spent a full cycle of the planet's moons in the desolate area. It was part of the training expected of anyone who wished to become a vryndarr.

"Funny how no one mentioned that little detail when we were volunteered to help with this mission." I was glad Celeste's anger was focused on Burke and not Laria. Burke might have negotiated the terms, but technically, Laria was the one who'd finally convinced her friends to help.

"Hey, you're being paid well for your time." Burke held up his hands palm out, then leaned back and locked them behind his head. "And it's for a good cause."

Laria rolled her eyes. "Speaking of causes, how do you plan to get us inside the ship without being seen by Doyle and his men?"

"I'm familiar with the layout of the interior passageways, the ones only the engineers had access to," Burke said.

"I thought you worked security. How do you know about those corridors?" The way Sloane posed the question made me wonder if she was familiar with the alternative access as well.

"After the crash, one of the engineers responsible for maintaining ship functions relocated with my group. During our time together, he explained the inner workings in great detail."

"Where is this male now? Why did you not bring him along to show us the way?" Zaedon asked.

Burke drained the last of his drink, a solemn expression on his face. "Because he died. He was killed shortly after the war started."

"I'm so sorry." Laria placed a comforting hand on Burke's arm.

"It was a long time ago, but thanks." Burke placed his

hand over hers, lingering longer than the normal connection between friends would dictate.

If there was more to their relationship than that of a working partnership, I was in no mood to witness it. The thought of them sharing a bed, of him seeing her naked and exploring what I longed to touch, set anger rippling through me. I controlled my unwanted irrational emotions by downing the remainder of my drink, and slamming the mug on the table harder than I had intended to.

"Everything okay, Jardun?" Zaedon asked, quirking a questioning brow, then perceptively glancing between Laria and me.

"Everything is fine." It was not like me to feel so unbalanced, so out of control. I feared if I remained in the room any longer, I would embarrass myself, or worse, attack Burke for my unproved suspicion. I rose from my seat to leave. "I suggest we retire. We have a long trip ahead of us."

Zaedon was halfway out of his seat when I clamped my hand on his shoulder. "Get some rest, my friend. I will take the first watch." I did not stay around to hear any objections, but hastily left the building.

***

Once I was outside with the door closed behind me, I inhaled several deep breaths to calm my irritation. I moved to the end of the platform, finding a place where I could observe the surroundings from within the shadows.

A few minutes later, the door opened and Laria slipped through the exit, her movements silent, stealthy. She had no reason to venture outside where it wasn't safe, and I immediately became suspicious. Had my instincts about the female been wrong? I remained unmoving, waiting to see what she would do.

"Jardun." She spoke into the cool evening air, her gaze scanning the area beyond the platform, then shifting in my direction as if she could sense my presence in the darkness.

"Here." I moved into the dim light peeking through the interior window coverings. "Why are you not retiring with the others?" I feared mentioning my desire to keep her safe would lead to an angry discussion about her capabilities. I enjoyed seeing the fire in her green eyes, but did not want it to be there because of an argument. I wanted it to be the result of my touch.

"I'm not ready to sleep and… You seemed upset." She bit her lower lip. "I thought you might like some company, maybe want to talk. But if you'd rather be alone, I can go back inside." She hitched her thumb toward the door.

I should have let her go, insisted she return to her friends. Instead, my wayward tail circled the back of her legs, ensuring she did not leave. "No, I would like you to stay…please."

She nodded. "Okay."

She didn't seem to mind having me hold her inches away from my body, but the warmth seeping through her pants was affecting my scales. I forced my tail away, severing our contact before my arousal became apparent.

She was an anomaly who'd saved my life. A fierce warrior wrapped in the guise of a beautiful female, and there was so much more I wished to know about her.

One of the first mandates Khyron had ordered after becoming our leader was for all those closest to him to view the data the Earthers had provided his father. He believed the best way to bring unity to the inhabitants of Ketaurrios began with understanding and accepting their differences.

I had been fascinated by human cultures and customs. I struggled with comprehending why some humans believed in fate, yet had been curious about the concept when I had come across it during my studies. I'd found similarities between their belief of love found at first sight and our belief of finding our mate by scent.

Many questions I had never considered before ran

through my mind. If fate existed, did it also play a role in choosing our future? There was a time long ago when finding a female, my ketiorra, and having a family was something I longed for. Before I could find the one female whose scent enticed me, I had been given the opportunity to join the vryndarr and protect the leader of my people. My ventures were risky, and other than having the company of the males, some of whom were my closest friends, being a warrior had become a solitary existence, not one meant to be shared with a female.

Had fate purposely put Laria in my path? No female, past or present, had ever stirred the heat within me the way she did. Could she be a part of my future, the one I'd dreamed about before the war, then afterward had given up hope of ever obtaining?

Her gaze locked with mine as if she could hear my thoughts. The moment was brief, and after showing me a hint of a smile, she broke the silence between us. "You're worried about the drezdarr, aren't you?"

For only being acquainted a short time, she was more perceptive than Zaedon. "That among other things."

"If Doyle has the antidote, we'll find it."

Her confidence was reassuring, had a calming effect, and helped ease some of my tension. "I hope you are right."

She leaned against the building's exterior, still close enough for me to touch.

After staring into the darkness beyond the platform, she shifted her gaze toward me. "Do you think the soldiers next door are working with Doyle?"

"It had crossed my mind." It wouldn't be the first time some of my kind had betrayed my people for personal gain. Sarus was a good example of what happened when someone let the need for power control their decisions. I did not know her well enough to share my private views about the male or my belief that he was still alive.

She tapped the fingertips of one hand against her thigh.

"I assume you're working on a contingency plan."

I smiled, impressed by her wisdom. "Not only are you a skilled warrior, but you think like a vryndarr."

"Was that a compliment?" She laughed. "For a mere female?"

"I am quickly discovering there is nothing simple about you." I tucked a lock of hair that had escaped her braid behind her ear. She sucked in a breath, trembling beneath my touch. Unable to resist the urge to taste her lips any longer, I covered her mouth with mine. It was a gentle brush against fuller, softer flesh, more enticing than the females of my species.

Her soft whimper and the way she pressed against my body encouraged me to place my hands on her hips and pull her closer. I deepened the kiss, my tongue caressing hers, a dance that had me yearning for more.

I was so consumed with Laria's response and the pleasure of having her in my arms that my mind barely registered the door opening and the interior light splashing onto the platform. I released her seconds before Burke stepped through the doorway.

"Jardun." His gaze swept from me to Laria, his brow furrowing. "Sorry, didn't mean to interrupt."

His irritated tone conflicted with his statement, making me wonder if he truly regretted his intrusion.

"I thought you'd want to know that I'll be taking the next shift. Wake me when you're ready." Burke spun on his heels to go back inside, closing the door behind him harder than necessary.

"I should probably..." Laria glanced at the closed door.

"Of course." I reluctantly released her hand. Encouraging her to stay, to continue what I'd started, was tempting. But allowing myself to get closer, to become emotionally attached to her, was a distraction I couldn't afford. Not with so many lives counting on me to make rational decisions.

CHAPTER EIGHT

LARIA

Years of dealing with unsavory elements had taught me to be a light sleeper. I'd gone to bed, my lips still tingling from Jardun's kiss, thinking about how he made me feel, and certain I wasn't going to get much sleep. Surprisingly, the two glasses of strong homemade brew I'd had with my meal had more of a relaxing effect than I'd expected. Even the slightest noise couldn't penetrate my deep slumber. When my groggy mind registered there was a hand clamped over my mouth, my first instinct was to scream. The second was to reach for the blade tucked under the clothes I was using as a pillow.

"Shhh, it's me," Sloane whispered before I could grip the handle. "There's something moving around outside." She tipped her head toward the pane near her bed, then removed her hand from my mouth.

Apparently, I'd missed a lot while I was out, and silently swore to avoid all forms of sensory-impairing drinks until after this trip was over. The handles of the blades Sloane had jammed against the panes earlier rattled, followed by some heavy scraping along the exterior frame.

It sounded as if someone was trying to pry one of the panes open from the outside.

I glanced toward Celeste's empty bed and saw the small dish of crystals she kept nearby. Their natural soft glow wasn't bright, yet gave off enough light to see the surrounding room. I never complained about them because I knew she used them to ward off nightmares. And, if I was being honest, I always found them comforting. "Where's Celeste?"

"Over here." She'd moved to the far corner and was reaching for her pants.

"What are you doing?" I couldn't figure out why she was taking the time to get dressed when preparing for who was trying to get through the window seemed more important.

"Going to get the guys." She finished tugging the pants to her waist, then headed for the door, grabbing one of her knives along the way.

Not a bad idea considering we couldn't see outside and didn't know for sure what was out there. The creatures Zaedon told us about immediately came to mind. After reminding myself they only inhabited the wastelands, I realized it had to be the males from the other building. And if it was the soldiers, then what had happened to the person from our group who was supposed to be standing guard. What if it was Jardun and something terrible had happened to him?

Since I'd tossed my timepiece in my bag when I'd stripped out of everything but my shirt before slipping into bed, I had no way of knowing what time it was or if one of the other males had taken over for him. If I hadn't been concerned with bruising Jardun's ego, I would have pushed him to let me help stand guard. Second-guessing my actions wasn't going to change anything, so I concentrated on the current situation.

The knife handle rattled again, the pane closest to Sloane shaking hard enough to loosen the blade. The handle end made a downward slide along the glass, then dislodged and dropped to the bed.

"Crap." Sloane grabbed the fallen knife, then climbed up on the bed and stood with her body pressed against the wall.

"Sloane, wait." I rushed back to my bed to retrieve my blade.

As soon as I turned, one of Tarzel's men shoved the wood panel closest to Sloane aside, then squeezed his large chest through the opening. I hadn't heard the outside pane break and assumed he'd removed a portion of the exterior wood to slide the glass easily from the frame.

His gaze widened. The shock of seeing Sloane standing next to the window, and not asleep in her bed as he'd expected, wore off in an instant. He moved fast, grabbing her wrist and squeezing hard.

Sloane cried out but refused to drop her knife. "Let go of me, you slimy lizard."

Because of her size, it was easy for him to wrap his other arm around her waist and pull her toward the opening. She grabbed the frame with her free hand and braced her feet on the wall, trying to remain inside.

No, no, no. I wasn't about to let him drag my friend through the opening. I sprang onto the bed and sliced his arm. Not enough to cause major damage, but enough to cause pain and make blood gush across his skin.

The male jerked, his loud, feral roar hurting my ears, his glare full of menace. He refused to let go of Sloane's waist, but released her wrist to swing at me. At the same time I dodged his hand, Sloane jabbed her knife into his chest below his shoulder. He bellowed even louder, then released Sloane and staggered backward as he gripped the hilt of the blade.

"What happened?" I heard Tarzel ask, then got a glimpse of him behind the guy who'd grabbed Sloane.

"The draeking females attacked me." The male yanked the knife from his chest, then took a step forward as if he planned to come through the window again.

It didn't take much imagination to know that sex was no longer the only thing they had planned for Sloane and me if they got us out of the building. I took a defensive stand on the bed's padding and tightened my grip on the knife. "This female is going to do more than slice your arm if you try to come in here again." I glanced at the lower part of his anatomy, ensuring he understood where I planned to start cutting if he was stupid enough to come after us again.

"Leave them," Tarzel ordered. "By now, the other males are aware of our presence and will be coming. We need to go." He took off without waiting for a response.

The male stood there clutching Sloane's blade, his chest heaving. After a moment of glaring at us with indecision, which I was sure involved exacting revenge, he growled, then followed Tarzel into the darkness.

"Hey, asshole." Sloane smacked the wall. "That was one of my favorite knives."

I shook my head. Leave it to my friend to be more worried about one of her possessions than the possibility of being injured. Burke and Zaedon appeared outside the window. "What happened? You two all right?" Burke glanced at us, then at the damaged frame.

Anger and the ferocious glint in Zaedon's dark turquoise eyes wasn't a look I'd seen on the easygoing ketaurran before. A solarveyor engine rumbled in the distance, drawing his attention. "Stay here," he told Burke, then slipped into the darkness with silent stealth.

Burke was used to being in charge but didn't seem annoyed with the order. He'd probably reached the same conclusion I had. Even if Zaedon made it to the transport, there was no way he could stop it.

"Laria!" Jardun yelled from the corridor seconds before bursting into the room with Celeste on his heels. He froze, his gaze taking in the smear of blood I'd gotten on my arm during the struggle. "Where are you hurt?" he asked as he scooped me into his arms, then perched on the edge of the bed with me settled sideways across his lap.

His hair was mussed, his pants the only thing covering his body. It was hard not to be distracted by the contours of his bare chest or remember how much I enjoyed the kiss we'd shared earlier. If we'd been alone, would I have minded his attentive behavior? Probably not, and that was the problem.

My attraction to him was more than physical. I was starting to care. Dealing with Doyle was going to be dangerous and I needed to stay focused. There was no room for emotional ties on this mission or in my life afterward. I knew better than to develop a personal attachment to a guy I hardly knew and would be walking away from once we returned to the city.

Since everyone was curiously watching our interaction, I had no intention of giving them a show or encouraging any more attention from Jardun. "I'm all right." I cupped his cheek to stop him from running his hands along my back and ribs checking for injuries. "It's not my blood, so you can let me up now."

His peered around the room, finally taking note of the others. "I…am glad."

He slowly lifted me off his lap, then lowered me to my feet as he stood. The movement hiked my shirt up even farther. As soon as he released me, I grabbed the hem and tugged it back down.

"I'm fine too, in case anyone was wondering." Sloane jumped off the bed and landed next to Celeste with a thump. They both grinned at me with one of their I-told-you-so looks.

I rolled my eyes. I wasn't about to give them the chance to add a smart remark about Jardun's attentiveness, at least not while he was standing in the room with us. "How's the wrist?" I set my blade aside, then took her hand and studied the band of red marring her skin.

Sloane twisted her hand back and forth, then flexed her

fingers. "It's not broken or anything, but I'll most likely have some bruising by morning." She nudged my shoulder. "Oh, and thanks for the save."

"No problem. I'm just sorry you lost your blade," I said.

"What did I miss?" Celeste asked.

"Oh, the usual." Sloane bobbed her head. "We got attacked by a bad guy, and Laria stopped him from pulling me out the window."

"Yeah, but Sloane stabbed him in the shoulder, and the annoying male took off with her knife before you guys got here," I added, then stepped around Jardun to grab my pants.

Celeste slapped her hands on her hips. "Well, darn, that's twice in two days I've missed out on all the fun." She glanced at Sloane. "Next time, you get to go for help."

Burke leaned through the opening, then snorted. "You three can save the congratulatory recap for later. Let's see about repairing this mess."

"Hey, has anyone seen Garyck?" Sloane glanced around the room, a hint of concern in her voice.

"He was on watch." Jardun turned to leave the room.

Sloane raced around him and collided with the hulking body now standing in the doorway.

Garyck placed his hands on her shoulders to keep her from falling backward. "Little one, you should watch where you are going."

Sloane shrugged away from his hold. "And you should learn to make more noise."

Garyck responded with a grunt, then turned to Jardun. "I was attending a fire near the outside of the storage building." He gazed at the damaged pane and shutter, the furrow on his brow deepening. "I assume the males used it as a distraction."

"As we suspected, they were after the females," Jardun said.

Sloane crossed her arms and proudly stuck out her

chin. "Don't worry, Laria and I made sure one of them will have a couple of scars to remember us by."

Garyck obviously didn't find her comment amusing. He clenched his fists, radiating tension. "We should have dealt with them when we had the chance." He snarled, then stalked from the room.

I had a feeling Garyck's idea of dealing with someone involved bodily injury. Based on the interaction between Jardun and the soldiers when we'd first arrived, I assumed the males had broken one or more ketaurran rules. Coming after us had only made things worse.

"Is he going to be okay?" Sloane asked Jardun.

"He…" Jardun gripped his nape. "Yes, he will be fine."

I moved behind Celeste to pull on my pants. Just as I finished, Zaedon appeared in the doorway. He seemed a lot calmer than he had when he'd gone after the other males. He took a few steps into the room and held out Sloane's blade, now free of blood. "The male dropped this on the ground. Who does it belong to?"

"That would be me." Sloane took the knife, then cradled it against her chest as if it was the only possession she owned. "Thank you so much."

"You are welcome." Zaedon's grin was short-lived. He turned to face Jardun. "The other males left before I could stop them. But I am afraid we have another problem."

"Which is?" Jardun asked, his tone laced with frustration.

"They disabled the energy absorption unit and the communication transmitter in our vehicle," Zaedon said.

"Does that mean we're stranded here?" Celeste asked.

"Stranded, no. Unable to use the transport to return to the city, yes." Jardun held up his hand. "We can discuss travel arrangements later, after we have repaired the pane and secured the building."

LARIA

"You've got to be kidding." Celeste had her back to me and was standing on the building's exterior platform near the open door.

"What's wrong?" I pulled a thin strip of leather into a tight knot around the end of my braided hair and walked outside to see what she was complaining about. After the evening's events, none of us had gotten a lot of sleep. My friend was even crankier than I was when she was exhausted.

Celeste threw her hands in the air and glared across the compound. "I can't believe they expect us to make the rest of the trip on those things." She pointed to the right where rows of fencing, cut from the thorny blue trunks of scaasean trees, were interconnected to form large pens. "They look like giant iguanas."

Inside the nearest enclosure, Zaedon and Garyck were securing what appeared to be seats with long straps around the midsection of the creatures Celeste had been talking about. They were a much larger version, closer to the size of a two-seater transport, of the Earth lizard I'd learned about as a child.

Now that the storm had stopped, I could see the entire outpost and the surrounding area. The three buildings, staggered closely together, had been constructed on top of a flat area of land composed of reddish orange sand. A mountainous wall of rock bordered it on two sides and provided natural protection.

After we'd discovered the solarveyor had been disabled and Jardun told us he had an alternate form of transportation, this was not what I'd expected.

"They might look like overgrown lizards, but they seemed friendly enough. I don't think you have to worry about them trying to eat you." I draped my arm across her shoulder. "Just think of it as riding a horse, only they're bigger and probably much slower."

"I've never been on a horse," Celeste huffed and bounced her hip off mine. "*And* not all of us are into the outdoor experience."

"It's too bad Cara didn't come with us. She'd have the transport repaired and running in no time," Sloane said as she joined us.

Cara was one of our friends who also lived in the settlement. She also worked for Burke and occasionally traveled with Celeste, Sloane, and me. She had amazing talent when it came to anything mechanical. There wasn't anything on the planet she couldn't fix. I hadn't seen her in several weeks and assumed she was spending time with her parents. The older couple lived on one of the outlying farms. Cara occasionally stayed with them to help with chores, mostly during the harvesting seasons.

Burke came out of the building and walked to the edge of the platform. "Laria's right. The chaugwai aren't flesh eaters, so you'll be perfectly safe."

Celeste shook her head. "I don't care about their eating habits, I'd rather walk back to the city than ride one of those things."

"How do you think the soldiers got them to stay in the pen?" Sloane asked. "There's no way they can't crawl over that four-foot fence."

"They fed them." Zaedon stopped the two creatures he'd been leading by the platform's edge. "As long as there is food, they will not leave the area."

"Okay, but why would anyone want to keep them around in the first place?" Sloane curiously eyed the creature.

Zaedon tipped his head toward the rocky ledges in the distance. "They can travel where a transport cannot."

"Speaking of transports, are you absolutely sure ours can't be fixed?" Celeste wrinkled her nose when the chaugwas swiped its long, thin yellow tongue across

Zaedon's forearm.

"If we were able to make the repairs, using the transport would add additional time to the trip." Zaedon rubbed the chaugwas's forehead, earning him another lick. "If the weather does not cooperate and we have more rain, the vehicle's energy will be drained, and recharging will cause more delays. Besides, it is no longer a good idea to travel the roads through the open areas. If Doyle has been warned about our presence, he will be monitoring the main access points and will see us coming."

"Which means we need another way into the wastelands," Burke said. "And these animals are good at scaling rocky ledges."

"Hold on. When you say scale, what exactly do you mean?" Sloane asked.

"Guess you'll see when we get there," Burke said, then flashed us one of his smart-assed grins. He shrugged his bag over his shoulder and stepped off the platform. "Get your gear. We need to get going."

I glanced from my friends to the chaugwai. "How bad can it be?" I tried my best to sound optimistic, but failed at keeping the wariness out of my voice.

"You mean besides the scaling thing? I'd say hours riding in those seats isn't going to be comfortable." Celeste crossed her arms and bobbed her head. "But hey, what's getting a few blisters near our girl parts when you compare it to saving lives, right?"

Her sarcasm wasn't lost on me, nor was the fact that she was still irritated with me for talking her into helping the ketaurrans. I hoped my zest for doing the right thing wasn't going to get us all painfully hurt, or worse—killed. "We knew what we were getting into when we agreed to help."

Sloane nudged Celeste from the other side, her gaze locked on Garyck. "I can think of something I'd much rather be doing with my girl parts."

Celeste's cough had me rolling my eyes and glancing

from one friend to the other. "Okay, so we didn't know about the giant lizards, but since we're here, we may as well get going."

I turned to go back inside to gather my gear, and ran right into Jardun's chest. It was like bouncing off a sturdy wall of flesh. I grabbed his arm to keep from stumbling backward. I had no idea how long he'd been leaning against the doorframe listening to us. If I based my guess on his inquisitive smirk, I'd say he'd heard our entire conversation, girl parts and all.

The heat searing a path along my throat and cheeks got even warmer. While I contemplated my recently acquired lack of coordination, he placed his hands on my hips. My ability to concentrate had diminished, and it took me longer than necessary to realize he wasn't letting go, and even longer to admit I enjoyed being held in his arms.

I forced the thoughts away, reminding myself again why caring wasn't a good idea and why I needed to keep things between us professional.

"Shouldn't you be getting ready, or doing some leader-type things, instead of lurking in doorways?" I asked.

He pressed his head to my cheek and spoke softly into my ear. "Probably, but then I would have missed your enlightening reference to the female anatomy." With a sniff of my neck, he released me, then stepped aside so I could enter the building.

What was it with the sniffing? I remembered how he'd done the same thing the first day we'd met. Ketaurrans had an enhanced sense of smell, and if he could smell my arousal, the last thing I wanted was for him to mention it loud enough for my friends to hear. Sloane was already relentless with her comments regarding him, and knowing how he affected me would just encourage her to increase her efforts. After deciding it was best not to ask or give my friend any additional encouragement, I rushed inside.

When I returned with my bag, Burke, who'd been helping prepare more of the chaugwai, was leading two more of them, and Garyck was following him with the other three.

"Do you suppose you could make the whatsa thingy move closer to the platform?" Celeste asked Zaedon as she waited for him to strap her bag behind the seat on the back of one of the animals. "I don't want to ruin my boots." She emphasized her request with a pitiful pout.

I was pretty sure I wouldn't earn any points if I reminded her about the other pairs she had stashed in my transport. I tried not to laugh when Zaedon growled because Celeste missed his shoulder and ended up pulling his hair in her less than graceful attempt to mount the chaugwas without stepping in the sandy mud.

Garyck stopped in front of Sloane, a hint of a smile curving one end of his mouth. "Perhaps you should remain behind."

Sloane crossed her arms. "Oh yeah, and why is that?"

"Because you will require constant assistance with mounting. We do not have time to waste helping a female who barely reaches the top of the chaugwas's hindquarters."

"Make one more wisecrack about my height and I'll shave those pretty golden locks from your head," Sloane sneered, then palmed the handle of the short-bladed sword sheathed on her hip.

"And how do you plan to do that, *little one*? You are not tall enough to climb on the chaugwas's back, let alone reach my head," Garyck said, then tapped her nose. Even standing on the ground, which was a good foot lower than the platform, he was taller than my friend.

Sloane rarely reacted the way anyone expected. Instead of getting angry, she tilted her head to the side and flashed him a mischievous smile, which I knew meant trouble. "You've gotta sleep sometime." She smacked him in the chest, then spun on her heel and launched herself toward the overly large lizard. She kicked off the creature's leg, then, in a graceful acrobatic move, used its neck to hoist herself into the seat.

She leaned forward and yanked the leather lead from Garyck's hand. "Are you coming, or do you plan to stand around with your mouth hanging open all day?" She tugged on the strap and dug her heels into the chaugwas's ribs, urging it to move forward.

Zaedon smirked, but before he could say anything, Garyck held up his hand. "Do not…"

After slinging my bag over my shoulder, I walked to the edge of the platform next to Garyck. He shifted his gaze away from Sloane long enough to acknowledge my presence with a nod.

It was hard to resist teasing the grumpy male, so I leaned closer and said, "Word of advice." I also thought he deserved to know what he was dealing with. I knew Sloane well, knew she was devious and had a reputation for following through on her threats.

He grunted.

"Sleep with one eye open." I chuckled, then stepped off the platform and plodded through the moist sand, following Jardun to the last two mounts.

CHAPTER NINE

JARDUN

The ride along the base of the mountainous border of the Quaddrien was slow and steady, the sky was free from any threatening storm, the heat from the sun's rays tolerable. I shielded my eyes and stared at the smooth flat surface of the rocky ridge, wondering what I'd been thinking. The last time I had crossed into the wastelands, I was young and willing to embrace all forms of peril. I did not remember it appearing quite so ominous. I knew the chaugwai wouldn't have any trouble climbing the wall, I was more concerned about the females being able to stay on their backs during the ascent.

The longer our group traveled, the farther we got from the outpost, the harder it was to deal with the overwhelming need to keep Laria and her friends safe. Maintaining rational thought had eluded me from the moment I'd tasted her enticing lips. The memories were fresh, the knowledge that relationships between humans and ketaurrans, though rare, were possible, had desire coursing from my core to the tip of my tail. Compounding my emotions were vivid images of seeing blood on her arm after the other males had attacked.

With the solarveyor inoperable, contacting Khyron or having the females return to the city was no longer an option. Not that the infuriating females would have followed my orders. After last night's attack, they seemed even more determined to reach Doyle's fortress and rescue Vurell.

My plan was to stay as close as possible to Laria whether she liked it or not. Feeling responsible for her safety because I had asked for her help on this mission was not the only reason I wanted to protect her. The more time I spent with her, the more physically and emotionally bound to her I became. Not for the first time since our paths had crossed did I wonder if it was possible for a human to be my ketiorra. More specifically, I questioned whether or not Laria was my true mate, the one female on the planet whose scent and nearness called to me like no other.

Now was not the time to analyze what might be between us or if pursuit of a joining would result in resentment from members of both our species.

I turned my attention back to the large rock wall, and scanned the terrain for a less imposing and easier way to reach the upper ledge that would take us into the desert area on the other side.

Zaedon pulled his animal to a stop next to mine, then glanced at the females. "I assume you would prefer finding a way to the top that did not include having to scale the exterior surface."

Every male in the vryndarr, every male I called friend, had fought by my side, had survived many deadly missions during and after the war. Zaedon was like a brother, knew me well, and very rarely needed me to explain what I was thinking. I was grateful he'd recognized my concerns for the females without making me state it out loud.

"It may be tight and a little steep, but it appears there is a ledge along the ridge that angles upward." He pointed to the right. "It would also minimize the time spent clutching the necks of the chaugwai."

"I agree." Garyck eased his animal to a standstill on my other side. "It will take a little longer, but there is less risk of injury." He glanced ahead of us to where Laria and her friends, including Burke, had climbed down from their mounts and were stretching their legs.

I urged my chaugwas toward the others, then addressed them as a group. "In order to reach our destination, we must go over this ridge." I angled my chin in the direction of the massive cliff behind us. "Zaedon will take the lead, followed by Celeste and Sloane. Garyck and Burke will position themselves in the middle, with Laria and myself following at the rear." If something should happen and any one of the females was to slip from her mount, then the males would be able to keep her from dropping to the ground below. As far as I knew, Burke did not have any experience climbing with a chaugwas, but I had witnessed his skills and was confident in his abilities.

Celeste tipped her head back, blocking the sun with her hand as she stared at the top of the ridge. "Jardun, there is no way my chewy thingy and I are going to be able to climb up there." She lowered her gaze and glared at him. "Maybe we should stay here and wait for you guys to get back." She gave a nervous laugh, and I was uncertain if she was attempting humor or being serious.

Luckily, Laria interceded before I could ask. "Since when are you afraid of heights?"

"Or anything else for that matter?" Sloane chimed in.

Celeste released an exasperated breath, then patted her chaugwas's neck. "Who says I'm afraid? I was worried about Lou getting hurt. What if he slips and sprains an ankle, or breaks a leg?"

"I don't know what's more troubling, the fact that you're whining worse than the time you got luzardee blood on your favorite pair of boots, or that you gave the damned lizard a name." Sloane shook her head, then jerked on the lead straps to follow Zaedon.

Burke chuckled, then smacked the rear end of Celeste's ride so it would start moving. "Get in front of me. I'll make sure nothing happens to Lou or you."

Laria waited for the others to pull ahead of her, then maneuvered her animal next to mine. "You've done this before, haven't you?"

"It has been many years, but yes," I said.

"Was it part of a dare? Because honestly, I don't understand why anybody would want to do this on purpose."

Her smile warmed me, had a calming effect that immediately put me at ease.

"It was a requirement when I chose to enlist in the vryndarr. But I am certain I have done many other things that you would consider a dare." As soon as her animal began to move, I tapped my chaugwas's ribs with the heel of my boot. "Perhaps one day when I am sure you will not think less of me, I may share them with you."

"We've all done things in our past we'd rather not share with anyone. But if you ever want to talk about them, I'm a pretty good listener." The trail narrowed, and she urged her chaugwas in front of me.

I did not think anything from her past equaled the dark things I had done to protect my people. Was I expecting too much from her comment, hoping that once this was over, I could entice her to remain in my world? It was a prospect I should not contemplate, had no right to expect, but quietly pondered anyway.

***

We followed the ridgeline as Zaedon had suggested, making good time with few incidents. Sloane's animal had slipped on some loose rocks, but she handled it well without being tossed from her mount. Garyck, who'd been staying closer to the female than necessary, looked as if he'd been holding his breath, and for a short time, the golden scales on his arms had paled to white. Perhaps he was more concerned about the female's welfare than he wanted anyone to believe.

The trail led us to the base of a sheer mountain face, the last remaining obstacle in reaching the ridge. When we stopped to give the chaugwai a break, Zaedon prepared Laria and her friends for the remainder of the climb.

"Secure the ends of the leads loosely like this." Zaedon tied the two leather straps together and secured them to the front of the seat. "Grip below the chaugwas's neck." He demonstrated by leaning forward and placing his hands on the animal's thick chest muscles. "This will keep you from sliding and allow him to breathe as he climbs the rocks."

"And what's going to keep Lou from sliding?" Celeste tipped her head to the side and glanced at the jagged rocks lining the basin below. "Or us plummeting to our deaths?"

"These mountains are part of their natural habitat. They are very adept at moving along the rocky surface." Zaedon gripped the front leg of his chaugwas, then bent its knee to expose the pad of its foot. He pressed his knuckles into the middle of the thick leathery layer, causing the skin to roll back and reveal several rows of hidden claws. "They use these to grasp the rock."

"You know that's not making me feel much better," Celeste said.

"Come on, Celeste. The guys will be right behind us." Sloane glanced at all the males in the group. "They won't let anything happen to us, will you?"

Celeste wrinkled her nose, clearly not reassured by our nods.

"Why don't I go first," Laria said. "If Zaedon isn't telling the truth and I fall, then you have my permission to avenge me any way you want."

Zaedon frowned. "Laria, I swear I would never…"

She giggled. "Relax, I'll be fine."

Of the three, Laria's will seemed to be the strongest. She was the one they looked to for guidance, the one they trusted. Though I heard a subtle strain in her voice, it did not deter her from the task. She winked at Zaedon, then urged her chaugwas toward the vertical wall of rock.

Following someone who knew what they were doing was one thing, scaling a sheer surface for the first time was another. It took all my restraint not to rush after her, to ensure nothing happened should she lose her grip. I was impressed by the way she followed Zaedon's instructions and allowed the animal the freedom to make its way upward. I wanted Celeste to be confident with the climb and waited until Laria was halfway to the top before trailing after her.

When I reached the ridgeline, Laria had dismounted and was waving to Celeste and Sloane.

She took in some deep breaths and smiled. "That was actually kind of fun, but I'm not in any hurry to do it again."

I quirked a challenging brow. "Not even on a dare?"

LARIA

Reaching the top of the ridge hadn't been an easy feat. My skin was coated in a sheen of sweat. My fingers were cramped, and my inner thighs throbbed from tightly gripping the chaugwas during the climb. The emotional exhilaration and fear pulsing through my body slowly subsided.

Heading into the unknown was never a good idea and something I rarely did without a little preparation. I'd believed Jardun and his friends when they'd said we could make it to the top safely. I'd been so focused on helping Celeste get over her fear that I hadn't given any thought to what might happen if I lost my grip and slipped from my animal's back. At least not until I was hanging halfway up the sheer rock wall, wishing I'd waited for one of the experienced riders to follow closely behind me.

Luckily, everyone made it to the top without any casualties, including Celeste, the reason for my daredevil performance. She was standing off to the side, talking to her newly adopted chaugwas and giving him an appreciative hug.

I climbed back on my animal, then urged him to cross to the other side of the flattened ridge so I could stare down at the Quaddrien. I'd been in my teens when the *Starward Bounty* had crash-landed on Ketaurrios. Memories of the trip I'd made with my father and the other families who'd been packed into a large solarveyor before being escorted from the wastelands filled my thoughts.

From up here, the Quaddrien looked completely different than it had all those years ago. It reminded me of a large bowl, a long, never-ending wave of reddish-brown sand surrounded on either side by a continuous rock wall, the center sprinkled with plant life in various shades of blue and purple. The area might hold many hidden dangers, but from up here, it was breathtakingly beautiful.

I wasn't surprised when Jardun stopped his chaugwas on my right. He hadn't been far from my side since we'd left the outpost. I'd been taking care of myself and looking out for my friends for so long that I wasn't sure how I felt about having a male constantly looking out for my safety. Though I'd occasionally caught him glancing in my direction, his gaze was currently focused on the horizon, and he appeared deep in thought.

I studied Jardun's profile. He was a true leader who held his team's respect. He exuded power, courage, and male prowess. And when he wasn't being an overbearing male intent on saving me because I was a female, I'd caught brief glimpses of a gentler side. A side I wanted to know.

It wasn't hard to guess what he was thinking about. "How long will it take us to reach Doyle's compound?"

"If we do not experience any delays, we should arrive

sometime tomorrow," he said.

I wondered what we'd find when we reached our destination, what Jardun would do if the doctor was dead and we couldn't find the antidote. They were questions I wanted to ask, but chose not to. I knew from experience that having hope and striving for a good outcome was the one thing that helped me survive.

Jardun already carried the weight of saving the drezdarr and, ultimately, his people. I wasn't about to diminish any hope he had about us being successful.

Zaedon's arrival put an end to any further discussion. "I have found an easy access to the basin below."

"Good. We will need to make good time if we want to reach the forest area by nightfall," Jardun said.

I leaned forward to see around Jardun so I could speak to Zaedon. "What, you're not going to make us hang on the side of a rock again and hope we don't drop?"

Zaedon chuckled. "I see why you like this female. Not only is she a skilled warrior with an intriguing scent, but her sarcasm is quite humorous."

He laughed even harder when Jardun growled. "I will inform the others," he said as he steered his chaugwas away from us.

"Care to explain about my intriguing scent?" I asked, hoping I'd inadvertently get an answer to the sniffing thing.

"No," Jardun replied defensively.

I couldn't hold back an amused grin when he muttered something about Zaedon needing to mind his own business, then turned his animal to follow the others.

Zaedon had been right about the ease of reaching the basin. The trail he'd found consisted of flat rocks eroded over time to form what looked like a long set of stairs.

Once we reached the bottom, Zaedon and Garyck took the lead, with Celeste, Sloane, and me in the middle, and Jardun and Burke following at the rear. Either the ketaurran males were normally suspicious or they were warily scanning the surrounding area because they expected some kind of danger.

It made me a little anxious, and I startled when Celeste appeared on my left and said, "That was a pretty bold move."

"Got your ass over the ridge, didn't it?" Sloane was pacing alongside me on the right.

"I was about to thank her before you butted in," Celeste grumbled.

The trip had already been long, I was exhausted and not in the mood to listen to my friends bicker. I knew they cared about each other, that arguing was their way of dealing with stress. Normally, I'd walk away, let them get their rants out of their systems. Since I couldn't walk, run, or ride away and had nowhere to go, I decided to change the subject.

My first thought had been to tease Sloane about Garyck, ask her if she really planned to cut off those golden locks in his sleep. The uncertainty of how she'd retaliate, possibly by openly discussing Jardun when he could overhear, made me select a neutral subject. "Once we get back to the city, what do you think about..." Celeste's chaugwas bolted forward before I got a chance to finish.

Celeste frantically yanked on the lead straps to make him stop. "What's wrong with Lou?" She rubbed his neck and cooed soothing words.

"And what's that noise?" Sloane asked as her animal pranced sideways.

I heard a loud rumble, the noise growing steadily stronger, the surrounding sand rippling from the vibration. Before I could investigate the source, my chaugwas bellowed. His anxious cry sounded like a combination of the deep base of a musical horn and severely loud snorts. He shook his head back and forth and spun in circles as if the pads of his feet were on fire.

"Easy there, big guy." No matter how much I tried to

soothe him or how hard I tugged on the straps, my chaugwas wouldn't budge from our current spot. He rocked back and forth, stomping the ground, the motion nearly unseating me.

"It is a snakkril. We need to move!" Jardun shouted, his voice barely audible over the deafening noise.

The ground five feet in front of my animal's head churned, the sand spinning and dropping to form a funnel with a smooth round object at its center. A dark copper-colored object that quickly transformed into the most hideous reptilian head with luminescent gold eyes I'd ever seen in my life. It hissed and growled, using short legs with claws along both sides of its snakelike body to push its way to the surface.

"What the…" My heart raced, the pounding in my ears almost as loud as the rumble I'd heard seconds earlier.

The snakkril used its coiled tail to propel it forward. I got a horrifying glimpse of its gaping jaws before it sank yellowish fangs as long as my fingers into the chaugwas's neck. My animal shrieked, his entire body shuddering as he reared up on his hind legs.

The straps were ripped from my hand, the leather burning my palm. I plummeted to the ground, landing hard on my back, the air whooshing from my lungs.

I'd barely inhaled a replenishing breath and rolled onto my hands and knees when Jardun yelled, "Laria, look out!"

I glanced over my shoulder. My chaugwas had toppled onto its side, the front of its chest covered with blood. The snakkril advanced toward me, its body undulating in a slithery crawling motion.

"Draeck." I pushed to my feet, my boots slipping in the sand until I hit solid dirt and stumbled forward. As soon as I was moving, I retrieved my sword, motivated by memories of those long fangs and the need to keep them from sinking into my back.

The creature had already demonstrated how fast it could move, and there was no way I could outrun it. The only chance I had was to turn around and fight. I swung my sword, the tip of my blade long enough to reach the creature's scaly skin without getting my arm clawed in the process. My first few defensive moves were lucky enough to leave several short gashes on the creature's underbelly.

"Burke, behind you!" Celeste called out.

Too afraid to take my eyes off the creature in front of me, I used my periphery to see what was happening around me. Two more snakkrils had emerged from underneath the ground and were heading toward the others in my group. The creatures were a quarter of the size of the one bearing down on me. Before they could attack the other chaugwai, Zaedon, Garyck, and Burke were on the ground, blades drawn and going after them.

Sloane and Celeste had stayed on their animals and sidled up next to the other chaugwai, grabbing the leads and doing their best to keep them from running away. It was bad enough my chaugwas was down, but if we lost the others, we'd be stranded out here on foot—a prospect I was certain none of us wanted to face.

The more I swiped, the more it snarled, each lunge more aggressive than the last. No matter how many cuts I left in its flesh, the disgusting thing wouldn't stop. It continued to snap its jaws and dodge my blows. With each horizontal swipe of my sword, the snakkril moved forward, and I took a step back. My foot slipped, and I went down. Before the creature could strike, Jardun grabbed its tail and yanked, then tossed it away from me. The second it coiled and lunged for him, he swung his sword, and the blade severed the snakkril's head from its body.

Jardun was hovering over me in seconds, bluish-green blood dripping from the end of his sword. He held his hand out to help me up. "Are you all right?"

"Yeah." I managed with a gasp, then gripped his wrist. I glanced toward Celeste and Sloane as he pulled me to my feet, relieved to see they were unharmed and had kept the chaugwai from running off. Garyck stood sentry close by, his sword held out defensively in front of him, the other two creatures decapitated, their parts scattered across the sand.

Blood trickled down Jardun's bare arm from several cuts. "But you're not." I reached for his arm to get a better look at the wound. "I need some medical supplies," I said, not directing my demand at anyone specifically.

"Laria, it will be fine. Their claws are sharp, but it is not deep." He placed his hand over mine.

His attempt to placate me wasn't working, and I snapped, "I don't care. I'm not taking any chances with it getting infected." I turned to Zaedon, who happened to be the closest. "Why are you still standing there? I need something to clean his wound."

He raised a brow, and, after receiving a nod from Jardun, he grinned and headed toward his chaugwas.

When Zaedon returned, he was carrying a leather pouch, which he handed to me. "You will find what you require inside."

I undid the tie and pulled out the contents. I wasn't sure if my hands were trembling because I'd survived becoming a meal, or if it was because I'd realized why my chaugwas had died so quickly. "The snakkrils are poisonous, aren't they?"

"Yes, but only a bite from their fangs is lethal."

Once I focused on the task, it didn't take me long to clean the cuts, then apply a medicinal salve and protective binding. After returning the supplies to the pouch, I met Jardun's gaze.

"Thank you." He curled his fingers over mine and applied a gentle squeeze.

"It's the least I could do after you saved my life." I pulled away, handed the pouch to Zaedon, then headed toward my downed chaugwas. I stared at the animal, saddened by its death. No creature should have its life ended in such a brutal manner, nor did it deserve to have its flesh slowly devoured by any of the wasteland predators.

Jardun wiped the blood from his blade by swiping it along the edge of my chaugwas's seat, then returned it to his sheath. "Its mate will no doubt be close by, so lingering would not be advisable."

"Are you saying there could be more of those things?" Celeste jerked her head, checking the ground around us.

"It is possible. They do not usually attack animals this big unless they get too close to their nests."

"*Nests*, as in multiple?" Sloane nervously glared at the ground.

"Do not worry," Zaedon said. "They do not usually build their nests this far from the rocky border because they prefer cool, damp soil. The heavy rains may be the reason they are out this far."

"Come on, there's nothing more you can do." Burke placed his hand on my elbow and aimed me toward his mount.

"Laria will be riding with me." Jardun stepped in front of us. His commanding tone left no doubt he expected his order to be followed.

Burke frowned and pursed his lips. I could tell by the way his grip tensed that he wasn't happy with the directive.

My emotions were still raw from the attack, and the last thing I wanted was to watch them demonstrate their dominance with an argument that could get physical. I'd trained with Burke enough to know he was highly skilled, but after watching Jardun fight, I knew he'd win. "It's okay, really." I nodded and gave Burke's arm a pat.

As soon as Burke stalked toward his mount, Jardun untied my bag. He walked over to his chaugwas and removed his as well. After tossing both bags to Zaedon, he held his hand out to me.

I'd been too independent and had taken care of myself for so long that refusing to comply with any male's demands was part of my nature. I knew by taking Jardun's hand, I'd be agreeing to a higher level of trust between us. After carefully considering how he'd risked his life to save mine, and knowing there was a part of me longing to feel those strong arms wrapped around me again, I took his hand. I didn't resist when he placed his hands on my hips and helped me onto his chaugwas.

He swung himself onto the animal's rump, then settled behind the seat with his thick thighs pressed against the back of mine. He reached for the strap and motioned for Garyck and Zaedon to take the lead. It still amazed me at how well the three of them synchronized their efforts without saying a word.

I couldn't get the image of my chaugwas out of my head or stop being concerned about the same thing happening to someone in our group. I glanced at him over my shoulder. "Do you think we'll run into anymore snakkrils?"

"We should be fine if we keep moving and stay on the hardened ground." He tucked some loose strands behind my ear. "Do not worry. We will keep a close watch and ensure that everyone remains safe."

Even with the heat from the sun's rays, his gentle caress warmed me and sent a shudder rippling across my skin. He wrapped his arm possessively around my waist, urging me to lean against his chest. "Rest if you need to. We will make camp for the night once we reach the loicryn."

"What is the loicryn?" In all the interactions I'd had with ketaurrans I'd never heard the term before and was curious.

"I believe you would call it an oasis."

"Are you talking about the colorful blue area we saw from the ridge that has trees?"

"Yes. We will find fresh water and many plants to feed the chaugwai."

Some of the tension eased from his body, and he encircled my ankle with his tail, making me smile. He definitely had a way of making me feel safe, so I took his advice, resting my head against his shoulder and closing my eyes. It wasn't long before the animal's pace, its steady sway, and my exhaustion lulled me into a relaxed state.

CHAPTER TEN

JARDUN

I relaxed into the chaugwas's lumbering pace and allowed Laria's nearness to calm me. After joining the vryndarr, there had not been room in my life for a female. Any companionship I shared was the result of a brief encounter where my sexual needs were sated. Jealousy was not something I was familiar with. Yet I had no doubt the emotion was responsible for my reaction to the way Burke comforted Laria.

My observations of their interactions, along with her surrendering kiss, had convinced my logical side that the male's interests were his alone. My emotional side struggled to accept the information. Even now, as she slept in my arms, I fought with the urge to pummel the male for touching her. Had she not agreed to ride with me instead of him, I was certain a continued conversation between Burke and me would have ended in physical altercation with both of us requiring medical repair.

My irrational behavior was troubling, and once again I questioned if there was a deeper connection between Laria and me, whether or not she was my ketiorra. And what would I do if she was?

"Your Laria is very brave." Zaedon had slowed his chaugwas to keep pace beside mine a short time ago and was finally getting around to sharing what was on his mind.

My Laria. Somehow, the words felt right, but I knew better than to hope they might be true. "Yes." I glanced down at her slumbering form, her head resting below my chin, her feminine scent tainted with the odor of battle and raising havoc with my senses. She had fallen into a deep sleep not long after we started our journey to the loicryn.

"A ketaurran female never would have battled a snakkril." The females of my race were not weak, but because of our culture's longstanding tradition whereby the males took on the protective roles, their skills lay in other areas. Areas that did not suit the lifestyle of a vryndarr, a male trained from a young age to be a soldier, a protector, and an assassin if required. A ketaurran female would never willingly venture into the Quaddrien. Yet Laria, knowing the risks were dangerous, possibly lethal, had still agreed to help me.

"Perhaps Khyron is right, that our world will recover and find strength in bringing both races together." Zaedon sighed. "Watching your female demonstrate her abilities has given me hope that I may one day find my ketiorra, one with the ability to fight by my side."

Females were always to be cherished, to be protected. It was the way of our people for centuries. Yet to hear Zaedon embrace the vision of a different future, one where the vryndarr did not suffer a lonely existence, once again had me thinking about my attraction to Laria.

What was it about her that I found so appealing? Her beauty? Her strength? Her loyalty?

In the short time since we'd met, I had developed an emotional bond to her, one that stirred feelings and desires I had never encountered with another female. As much as I wanted this mission to be over, to have Khyron's health restored, I dreaded its conclusion. I had resigned myself to the fact that Laria would return to her life and I to mine.

Instinctively, I tightened my grip around her waist. Was it possible that the future held more than the singular goal of protecting the drezdarr and my people? Could she be the key to another path, one filled with the possibility of love?

The others slowed their animals. We had arrived at the edge of the loicryn, cutting my contemplations short.

"Remain here," Garyck said to Celeste and Sloane before handing his lead to Burke. In a smooth, precise move, he slid from the seat, his blade drawn before his feet touched the ground.

Zaedon handed me his lead, then dismounted and quickly followed after Garyck. Their goal was to survey the area and ensure it was safe before we entered and set up camp. Within minutes, they reappeared, Garyck signaling me with a hand motion that it was safe to proceed. Zaedon approached and took the lead for his animal.

The change in the chaugwas's motion caused Laria to stir. I tipped my head, grazing her ear. "It is time to wake. We have reached our destination."

"Um, okay." She groaned and wiggled to sit up, then tipped her head from side to side, stretching her neck. She glanced at the expanse of plant life in front of us: trees, grasses, blossoms in varying shades of blue, purple, and orange. She shifted sideways to give me a wry smile. "So this is what a ketaurran oasis looks like. I'm surprised anything this beautiful exists in the Quaddrien. I only got glimpses of sand and rocks from the inside of a solarveyor when we were relocated to the settlement."

I viewed the area, trying to see it through her eyes. Other than an overgrowth of tall grasses and the additional height to some of the trees, the area had not changed much since my youth. I remembered the days long ago when the handful of males who had joined the vryndarr, Zaedon, Garyck, and myself included, had completed a portion of the training and been thankful to reach the lush area.

The masters in charge were merciless in their survival teachings, setting our tasks during the hottest temperatures and worst conditions. A few hours spent in the cool shadows beneath the trees and quenching our thirst from the natural bubbling ponds had been a gift.

I slipped from the chaugwas's rump, then held out my hands to Laria. She pursed her lips as if to say she was capable of dismounting herself, yet placed her hands on my shoulders and allowed me to help her from the seat. I enjoyed the feel of her body pressed against mine and lingered with my hands on her hips longer than I should have.

"You guys coming?" Celeste asked, then shot Sloane an annoyed glare after the other female smacked her arm.

I was unsure what had transpired between the females, but it brought a hint of red to Laria's cheeks. "We should go."

"Yes." I reluctantly released her.

After everyone removed their bags from their animals, Garyck led us through some thick foliage to the clearing where he'd chosen to make camp.

Sloane kicked at the tall grass surrounding her feet, then squinted in Garyck's direction. "Not to criticize your choice of places to spend the night, but the blanket sleepers we brought aren't going to do much good if it rains."

"Not to mention keeping out any of the little creatures squirming in the dirt," Celeste added.

"We will not be sleeping on the ground." Zaedon walked over to some large blue fronds with streaks of purple running along the veins.

He pushed aside the giant leaves, exposing a large, cavernous area naturally formed within the trunk of the trees. It was wide enough for three or four people to sleep comfortably. Or at least as comfortably as anyone could on the hard, partially flattened surface.

"There are several of these hidden within this area." Zaedon grinned at Celeste. "Do not worry, zyrdena. You will not encounter any squirming creatures inside."

"You know, Zaedon"—Celeste placed her hands on her hips and straightened her shoulders—"Sloane's not the only one who knows how to shave someone's head while they sleep."

He snorted, letting the leaves drop back into place. "Are all human females as amusing as you?"

Celeste's face reddened, her fingertips toying with the handle of her blade. "I'll show you…"

"Okay, then." Laria stepped between them and hooked her arm through Celeste's. "Why don't we go find a place to sleep?"

LARIA

Because of the flat terrain, any fire used for warmth or cooking could be seen from a great distance across the wastelands. Jardun didn't want Doyle detecting our presence, so our evening meal had consisted of dried rations Zaedon found when he'd raided the storage building back at the outpost.

The compartment inside one of the tree trunks wasn't exactly comfortable, but it did provide Celeste, Sloane, and me with a cozy shelter. I rolled onto my side and listened to the heavy breathing coming from both of my friends. As usual, Celeste's stones weren't far from her head. I'd expected having to spend this much time around the ketaurrans would dredge up old memories for her and was glad to see her resting peacefully.

Sleep eluded me, and my body pulsed with energy. The nap I'd gotten earlier had refreshed the exhausted state of my body. I couldn't explain why spending time in Jardun's arms felt perfect, right, safe.

Afraid my restlessness would wake my friends, I

carefully pushed aside the leaves covering the entrance and slipped outside. The air was cool yet refreshing. Even with half of their rounded edges cast in shadows, the planet's two moons filled the evening sky with light. A light that gave the surrounding plant life a soft blue glow. Burke had taken an alcove not far from ours. I could hear his rumbling snore as I crept by.

I didn't have a particular destination in mind, but wasn't surprised when I arrived in the same clearing as Jardun. It was as if I had a natural ability to sense and home in on his presence.

He was sitting on the edge of a large boulder, staring at the horizon. The moonlight glistened along the scales on his arms and tail, making their pale blue surface shimmer. His bag sat on the ground near his feet, an indication that he had yet to select a place to sleep.

His head jerked in my direction, the hand covering the hilt of his sword immediately relaxing. His concerned frown was replaced with a smile. "Laria, why are you not with the others?"

"I couldn't sleep." I perched on the empty space next to him. "Are you still on watch?"

He shook his head. "Zaedon already relieved me, but I could not sleep either."

"Were you thinking about tomorrow, worrying about what we'd find?" *Or whether we'll be able to get out alive once we make it inside the ship?*

He shifted to face me, his gaze darkening and locking with mine. "No." He cupped my cheek, grazing my lower lip with his thumb. "I was thinking about you."

"Me… Why?" The moment he pulled me into his embrace and his lips captured mine, all other thoughts disappeared from my mind.

His growl was feral, his kiss possessive, more demanding than our last. It was as if he was staking a claim, one I was more than willing to accept.

"*Ketiorra.*" The soft words murmured against my lips

were barely more than a whisper.

Had he really called me his mate? My breath hitched, my pulse raced, my core heated.

He grazed the column of my throat, lavishing my skin with gentle kisses. "Share my bed with me tonight."

His request sent a shiver tingling along my spine. Even if it was only for one night, I wanted to be with him, to caress his skin, his scales. To run my hands over his firm body. To know what it felt like to have him inside me. "Yes," I gasped.

Another growl vibrated from deep within his chest. He lifted me off the ground, and I wrapped my legs around his waist, rubbing against his hard shaft and eliciting a groan.

With one arm keeping me in place, he leaned forward to grab his bag. He carried me to an alcove far enough from the others so we wouldn't be heard. He pulled the leaves aside, then gently set me on the edge. After I scooted farther inside, he tossed in his bag and climbed up next to me. The moonlight filtered through the leaves, providing dim lighting.

In a matter of minutes, he'd used his blankets to make a bed and taken off his vest and folded it into a pillow. After removing first his boots, then mine, he braced his back against the smooth trunk and pulled me onto his lap. He tugged the end of my braid. "I wish to see what your hair looks like when it is not bound."

I nodded my permission, then held his gaze as he tugged on the binding.

He slipped his fingers through the strands, slowly pulling apart the braid until the lengths cascaded over my shoulders. "I like it this way." He gave a curl an absent tug, then reached for the ties securing the front of my vest. Starting at the top, he peeled back the fabric, leaving a blazing trail of heat wherever his thumb touched my skin. By the time he'd bared my breasts, I was shuddering with need.

"There is no other creature on all of Ketaurrios that possesses your beauty."

Before his words could register, his lips were on mine, tasting and teasing, using his tongue to possessively take control of the kiss. At the same time, he splayed his hand along my ribs, moving upward to cup my breast. He brushed his thumb across the nipple, and I moaned. The warmth from the midday sun was nothing compared to his heated touch or the effect it was having on my body.

After grasping the hair at my nape, he tipped my head backward, using his arm to brace my upper body as he scorched a trail with his lips, moving downward from my shoulder. When he curled his tail around my ankle, I couldn't resist running my fingertips along its length, the scales flat and smooth to the touch.

Jardun shuddered and groaned, then tugged on my wrist. "My tail is extremely sensitive to stimulation. If you continue your caresses, I will explode like an inexperienced male."

"Really." I smirked. "Does that mean you're sensitive here as well?" I playfully swiped a path across the scales on his breastplate, then held back a satisfied grin when he sucked in a breath.

"Female," he growled, then grabbed me around the waist, rolling me onto my back with his hips wedged between my thighs.

"Laria," I corrected, then reached for him again, only to have my arms pinned above my head with one hand. Everything about him exuded power and control, and I wasn't surprised to discover it extended to his seduction skills. I found that I liked his dominant behavior, that it aroused me even more.

"Let us see how you like being teased, *Laria*." He purred my name, then cupped one breast, giving it a squeeze before lowering his mouth over the other.

The man definitely knew what he was doing. Switching between sucking and swirling his tongue, he transformed the nipple into a hard nub. It wasn't long before he had pleasure spiking from my core. "Jardun." I rubbed against his erection, frantic to have him inside me.

"Not yet," he murmured with a nip to my skin.

The more I begged, whimpered, and bucked, the more relentless he became in his ministrations to fulfill his promise of taunting. He kept my arms pinned, then slipped two fingers inside me, slowly pumping, each thrust pushing me closer to the edge.

He soon found the spot that sent my senses into overload and had me squirming even more. Not long after that, my orgasm hit, one rippling explosion after another, wrenching his name from my lips.

When I thought I couldn't take any more, thought I was about to pass out, he replaced his fingers with his cock. Each push and pull from his much larger shaft stimulated sensitive spots within me, hurling me toward another orgasm. One I was certain would be bigger than the last. One that might possibly kill me.

Several more hard and fast thrusts pushed me over the edge into ecstasy with Jardun following right behind me. We lay there, covered in a sheen of sweat, panting and trying to gain our breath.

When Jardun finally moved, it was to take a long-drawn-out sniff of my neck.

"Zaedon mentioned my scent earlier. Is there something wrong with the way I smell?" Since I hadn't bathed since the day before, I hated to think he found my odor unappealing.

"There is nothing wrong with the way you smell." He took another long inhale and rolled onto his back, pulling me close to his side.

"So why do you keep sniffing me?"

"The males of my kind are drawn to the scent of their chosen, their life mates." He adjusted his vest underneath his head.

"And?" I used his shoulder as a pillow and draped my

arm across his chest.

"And, it is time to get some rest." He closed his eyes and snuggled me closer.

Apparently, the frustrating male was done answering any more of my questions.

CHAPTER ELEVEN

JARDUN

I delighted in waking with Laria's body entangled in my embrace, strands of her golden hair splayed across my chest. It was a pleasurable experience, one I wished to prolong but knew was not possible. The first light of the sun's rays peeked through the gaps in the leaves, and it was nearing time to leave.

Zaedon must have known Laria was with me; otherwise, he would not be tromping around and making more noise than a chaugwas in heat.

"I take it someone is trying to get your attention?" Laria opened her perceptive green eyes and propped her chin on my chest.

"Zaedon." I ran my fingertip along the silky skin of her arm. "Garyck would not hesitate to interrupt us."

"I guess we should be thankful that Zaedon was up first, then." She winked, then leaned forward and nipped my chin.

I pushed several locks behind her ear and pressed a kiss to her forehead. "Laria, I…" *I what?* I did not want to let her go, but what could I say? I could not tell her I wished for a life together. I had no idea if any of us would survive the day. And if we did, then what? What kind of life could I offer her? I was a warrior, bound to protect the drezdarr, to protect my people as well as hers.

Her smile faded. "I know." She pulled from my arms, then rolled onto her hands and knees and reached for her clothes.

With a disappointed groan, I forced myself to do the same.

Shortly after I emerged from the alcove within the tree trunk, I spotted Sloane entering the clearing carrying two bags. I assumed one belonged to Laria.

Sloane dropped the bundle at her feet. "Has anyone seen… Oh." She grinned when I held the leaves away from the alcove's opening so Laria could exit behind me. I would be the first to admit that I did not understand the ways of human females, but was glad to see that at least one of Laria's close friends approved of our night spent together. Celeste appeared a few moments later. And though she appeared hesitant, she offered Laria a supportive smile.

If any of the males disapproved, they kept their comments to themselves. Burke might have been silent on the subject, but his irritated behavior and cool demeanor were indications that he was upset.

After a quick meal of rations and preparing the chaugwai for travel, we left the loicryn behind and used the nearest ridgeline to complete the remainder of our trip. We made better time than I had expected and reached our destination before midday.

Leaving the chaugwai a short distance away, we moved in a crouch to the rocky ledge overlooking what remained of the Earthers' spacecraft.

"To tell you the truth, I'd expected to see signs of Doyle's men long before now." Burke set his bag on the ground, then flattened his body next to an outcropping of rocks to get a better look below.

"It is possible that they arrived after we left and started searching the other outlying outposts, as we intended," Zaedon said.

When I had devised the plan, I knew the odds of it working were not in our favor. So far, taking the direct route over the ridge into the wasteland seemed to be successful. It did not explain the uneasy feeling creeping through my system.

Burke reached inside his bag and pulled out a medium-sized pouch. "I figured these might come in useful on this trip." He opened the pouch and retrieved an object that resembled two thin cylinders joined in the middle by a small piece of metal.

"Where did you get the viewers?" Celeste grabbed them out of his hand and held them up to her eyes.

"I acquired them from another Earther." Burke held out his hand and wiggled his fingers until she returned them.

"Don't you mean you confiscated them without paying for them?" Sloane asked.

"No, I believe that's your area of expertise." Burke smirked. "A guy owed me a few cradassons and couldn't pay, so he gave me these instead."

"What else have you got in there?" Sloane rolled on her knees and reached for Burke's pouch.

Burke snatched it from her hand. "Nothing you need to see, touch, or abscond with."

Sloane harrumphed, then crossed her arms. "Well, you're no fun."

"I'm a lot of fun, but I'm rather fond of my belongings and would like to keep them."

"May I?" Laria waited for Burke to give her the viewers, then turned and handed them to me. "These will magnify the view and make everything appear closer. Hold them with the smaller end to your eyes and point them at whatever you want to see. You should be able to get a better look at the ship's exterior and the entrance. You should also be able to see how many guards Doyle has posted."

"You have done this before?" I asked.

Laria smiled. "Once or twice."

I knew very little of her past, but becoming skilled at what she did took practice. I would bet she had been in similar situations more than two times, but refrained from stating my opinion. I held the viewers as she had instructed, and watched the world in front of me change focus. I was amazed at the clarity and detail.

I had not been a part of the old drezdarr's emissary group who had greeted and initiated the rescue of the humans. I had seen several pictures of the vessel taken before their exploring expedition began, and shared via the data sources the survivors had provided to Khyron and his father.

The vessel was much larger than I'd imagined, and from this viewpoint, the majority of the hull appeared to be intact. The portion closest to the bottom of the rock wall was partially covered with drifted sand. The rumors that Doyle had turned the vessel into his personal compound were accurate. "I count five transports, including the one the human male Rick used when he left the outpost." They were all situated in an area to the left and not far from the large space vessel. "I do not see the solarveyor used by the soldiers."

"Perhaps our assumptions that they were working with Doyle were incorrect," Zaedon said.

"It is possible they served under Sarus during the war, then maintained a pretense of loyalty to the drezdarr afterward to escape punishment." Disdain filled Garyck's tone.

My friend rarely shared his views, but I was aware of the emotional and physical scars he had received in connection to that particular subject. "It is possible they simply abandoned the outpost for fear of being imprisoned for attempting to steal the females." My chest tightened. I glanced at Laria and was reminded of how differently the events of that evening could have gone.

"Are there any guards posted outside?" Burke asked.

I tilted my head slightly so I could see the area on the opposite side of the vessel. Several males meandered along the perimeter. They appeared heavy in conversation, their demeanor indifferent, leaning toward boredom. "There are three armed with swords." I lowered the viewers and returned them to Burke.

He moved away from the ledge, then squatted near a smooth area in the loose sand and used the tip of his blade to draw a diagram. "From what my friend told me, the ship has an access entrance close to the point where the ship butts up against this rock wall. There's a lot of damage, but we should be able to use it to get inside. From there, locating the engineering level shouldn't be a problem."

Burke tapped a spot on the outer edge of the circle he'd drawn. "The lifts won't be operational, so we'll have to use the tunnels to reach the upper levels."

"What about finding Vurell and the antidote?" I pushed aside the overshadowing dread that we might already be too late to save the physician's life.

"That's where the girls come in," Burke said.

Sloane cheerfully bobbed her head. "The three of us"—she pointed to include Celeste and Laria—"used to play in the ducts when we were kids. If the antidote is anywhere on that level, I'll be able to extract it for you."

"I do not understand," Garyck said. "How do you plan to accomplish the task without being caught?"

"Let's just say I've always had a talent for acquiring things." She wiggled her fingers with a mischievous grin.

Garyck frowned and slapped his hand over his armband.

"You need to stop making that grumpy face." Sloane tucked her arms across her chest. "If I was going to take your precious piece of jewelry, I would have done it already." She waggled her brows. "Besides, there'll be plenty of opportunities during the trip back to the city."

Garyck snorted. "We shall see."

Not one to be dissuaded, Sloane jutted her chin. "Yes, we will."

"If you two are done…" Burke glanced at each member in the group, his gaze contemplative as if taking his time to choose his words. "Whatever we do, we need to do it carefully and be prepared for anything. The swords the males outside are carrying might be for show. There's a good chance that the ones inside are armed with weapons other than blades." He returned his knife to its sheath.

"What are you talking about?" Laria pinned Burke with a glare.

"There were cases of laser pistols and blasters stored on the ship. The Earth exploratory council kept it classified. Only certain members of the security team were given the information. Doyle was one of them. If the weapons survived the crash, there's a good chance he may have salvaged them."

"You bastard." A sob tore from Celeste's throat. "All these years you knew we had a way to protect ourselves from the attacks, to save people we cared about, and you didn't tell us."

Burke said, "After the crash, those of us who returned to salvage what we could weren't able to access that area of the ship. I thought everything in those storage areas had been destroyed."

"So what makes you think that's changed?" Sloane asked.

"A few months ago, I ran into some mercs I occasionally do business with. One of them got drunk and was bragging about how Doyle had taken over the vessel and some of the things he found. The weapons were mentioned."

"Why didn't you tell us then so we could have done something about it?" Laria asked.

"I was afraid if I said anything, the three of you would have come out here and tried to stop Doyle on your own."

"Of course, we would have," Celeste said.

"That's my point." Burke puffed out a heavy sigh. "I had no way of knowing if the information was accurate, and I wasn't willing to risk any of you getting killed over a rumor. But now that we're here…"

"We can find out if your associate was telling the truth." I shared a knowing glance with Zaedon and Garyck. Swords were no match against laser pistols. If the weapons existed, they would need to be destroyed. If there was a chance that Sarus was still alive, or if any of those loyal to him found a way to obtain the advanced weaponry, many more ketaurrans, as well as humans, would lose their lives.

"Was volunteering us to help Jardun an excuse to get your hands on the weapons?" Laria clenched her fists, her cheeks flushing.

"Hey, just because the war is over doesn't mean we can afford to be lax. Sarus hated our kind, and he had a lot of followers, some who would do anything to get rid of the current drezdarr. How long do you think we'd survive under their leadership?"

The fact that my friend was slowly dying from poison was proof of his statement.

The brief hint of regret on Burke's face was quickly replaced with irritation. "So, yeah, I'll do whatever it takes to keep all of us breathing, even if it means not disclosing important information."

Burke and I might share a common goal, but it did not mean I approved of his methods. And neither did the females—the evidence was apparent on their angry faces. He had not been forthcoming with me and he'd betrayed the trust of his friends. I would not be opposed, or stand in the way, should Laria decide to exact some retribution for his actions.

"We're definitely going to finish this discussion later,"

Laria said, then redirected the conversation back to the mission. "Do you have any suggestions on how we should avoid getting shot?"

"Don't attract attention, and don't get caught," Burke said.

"Yeah, that was helpful," Sloane grumbled.

"Let's say everything goes the way you planned with the rescue. How are we going to get back to the city?" Laria asked. "We obviously can't use the chaugwai again. Doyle's not going to let us leave without a fight, and they can't outrun gunfire."

"While you find the doctor and the antidote, Celeste and I are going to acquire one of those transports." Burke gestured toward the ledge.

With three males guarding that side of the vessel, I was not sure I agreed with Burke's plan. "Why take Celeste? Why not Garyck or Zaedon? They are much stronger and better equipped for battle."

"It's not strength he needs." She flicked her hair over her shoulder and smiled. "It's a distraction."

LARIA

After removing everything from the chaugwai, we gathered our bags and prepared to make our way down the rocks to the sandy surface below. Of course, we had to wait a few extra minutes so Celeste could say goodbye to Lou. She would never admit it—and would usually throw a punch at anyone who commented—but she had a soft heart when it came to animals, even if the creatures were the lizard variety.

Traveling to the basin was slow. Some of the ledges were narrow, others steep. Some portions lacked any kind of cover, and we were lucky we made it to the area near the tail end of the ship without being seen by any of Doyle's men.

So far, things seemed to be progressing smoothly. We

had a decent plan for getting inside, for reaching the lab, but it was the unknown that had my senses tingling. My internal warning system, the instinct that made my skin itch with dread, had been buzzing from the second we started our descent along the ridge.

I continually glanced toward the corner of the large vessel that wasn't buried in sand, expecting to see an unfriendly welcome party.

Burke interrupted my thoughts when he spoke to Jardun. "Celeste and I will stay here, give you time to reach the labs before we take out the guards."

"Zaedon, I want you to remain behind with Burke in case more males arrive and he requires assistance." Jardun issued the order in a tone that refused discussion.

I wasn't sure if his decision revolved around being a protective male, or if he didn't trust Burke any more than I did at the moment. Celeste could handle herself in any situation, but the vulnerable side she kept hidden sometimes appeared at the worst possible times and led to trouble. I was relieved that Zaedon would be staying behind to look out for my friend's safety.

Having an additional person outside meant we'd have backup in case things went badly inside. From what I'd seen since we started this mission, I knew the bond of loyalty between the three vryndarr was strong. Zaedon would never leave without his friends.

"Fair enough." Burke turned to me. "Once you get inside the passageway, the access entry to the tunnels should be to your right. From there, you can take it to the upper levels and find the lab."

It was a good thing this portion of the ship hadn't suffered much damage; otherwise, getting inside without security codes would've been a problem. Fortunately for us, the exterior hatch wasn't completely sealed. The thick metal edge was warped in a few places leaving a gap between the seal and the hull of the vessel. Ketaurran males were much stronger than humans, but I didn't realize how much until I watched Jardun and Garyck pry open the exterior hatch without breaking a sweat.

"Laria," Burke said.

I paused in the entryway and glanced at him over my shoulder. "Yeah."

"You guys be careful."

Mistrust and the sting from being used again would take me some time to get over. His concern for our safety might be genuine, but it was a little too late in the delivery. "That's the plan." I turned and followed Jardun, meeting up with Garyck and Sloane who were already inside and waiting for us.

We'd left our bags outside, but Garyck had retrieved a portable glow emitter before entering the ship. The small device contained several pieces of zapharite. The stones, used to absorb solar energy, gave off a blue-green glow and produced plenty of light to see down the long corridor in front of us.

It was obvious from the thin layer of untouched sand and dirt coating the floor that no one had been in this area of the ship for years. We continued along the passageway until we reached the first metal support beam

"This should be it." Sloane pointed at the faded red lettering painted above a panel on the wall that said "Authorized Personnel Only." After leaning forward and retrieving a thin knife from her boot, she used the blade to remove the fastening screws holding the vertical rectangular panel in place.

Once Sloane set it aside, Garyck placed a hand on her arm to stop her from going inside. "I will go first."

"Seriously, you're going to pull the overprotective male thing with me?" She returned his glare.

Sloane was tough and rarely backed down from anything or anyone. I was about to mention that we didn't have time for a battle of wills, when she stepped aside. "Fine, oh big and scary one." She made a wide sweep with her hand. "You can go first."

To me, Garyck's snorts sounded a lot like his grunts. I thought they were simply noises he enjoyed making.

It seemed Sloane had the ability to interpret their meaning. "Don't you *female* me, you cantankerous oversized lizard," she said as she climbed in behind him.

The inside of the tunnel seemed more confining than I remembered, and I was glad I wasn't claustrophobic. Of course, back then, I'd been a lanky teenager without the additional muscle and curves on my hips. "This brings back memories," I said to Jardun as I reached for the next rung in the ladder. Voices carried, and since I didn't want to alert anyone to our presence, I kept mine low.

"How so?" His hand brushed the outside of my thigh. He'd been in my personal space, never far from my side, since we'd started the climb. Not that I minded. After spending a night in his arms, I continued to crave his nearness. Remembering our evening of pleasure also brought a pang of sadness. I had no regrets about our time together, but falling for him was a bad idea, one that could only end in heartbreak—mine.

What I did, the risks I took, was hard on a relationship. It was why I'd never gotten involved with anyone. Jardun might believe I was his ketiorra, but it didn't guarantee a future together.

I tamped down the disconcerting thoughts, then paused to tighten my grip on a rung before glancing at him over my shoulder. "I've been in the engineering tunnels before, but never this far down in the ship. Mostly the ones near the labs."

Confusion furrowed his brow. "Why would you purposely want to be in such a cramped area?"

I understood why he asked. His broad shoulders were inches from touching the walls on either side of us, and he probably felt confined. "Let's just say Celeste, Sloane, and I weren't always good at staying out of trouble when we were younger."

He chuckled. "It does not appear that things have

changed much since then."

His attempt at humor warmed me. The risks he'd seen me take over the last couple of days were far bolder than any of my teenage antics. "I would have to agree with you."

CHAPTER TWELVE

JARDUN

Using the tunnels was not the first time I had experienced discomfort at being in a confined area. During the war, infiltrating tight and uncomfortable places overtaken by Sarus's males was commonplace. Though I enjoyed the constant view of Laria's backside, I was greatly relieved when we arrived on an upper level where we could utilize a passageway.

I thought about the exquisite night I had spent with Laria in my arms and knew with my entire being that she was my ketiorra. Over the last few days, I had witnessed her fighting abilities and she had earned my respect. It did not mean I would stop doing everything possible to protect her. I did not know what dangers awaited us once we reached the labs. After instructing Garyck to take the lead, I stayed at the rear of our group, so we could ensure the females remained between us.

"Is anyone besides me surprised that this level has power?" Laria paused in the middle of the passage, her gaze focused on the illuminated panels running along the metal floor.

"Is that a problem?" I asked.

"Actually, yes." Sloane glanced at me over her shoulder but kept walking. "These shouldn't be functioning. The loss of power and communications was a big problem after the crash. It was one of the topics the council members discussed with all the families before everyone was relocated."

"It appears someone has discovered a way to make the power work." It was fascinating to witness the human technology I had only read about. Had we been in a different, less threatening situation, I would have asked more questions about their functionality.

Sloane frowned and shot Laria a sidelong glance. "Makes you wonder what else we're going to find, doesn't it?"

"Yeah," Laria answered with trepidation.

When it came to technology, humans were far more advanced than my people. While some of their inventions were admirable, such as this space vessel capable of traveling to other worlds, there were other, more treacherous things I feared. The ability to design deadly weapons and toxins were at the top of the list.

"Which way?" Garyck slowed his pace. The passageway ended by connecting with two new corridors, one leading to the right, the other to the left.

"I'm pretty sure the labs are on the right." Sloane scooted past Garyck.

"Little one," Garyck growled under his breath when she ducked away from him and eased toward the adjoining passageway.

Sloane's movements were quick and silent. She held a finger to her lips, then knelt on the floor, pressing her body against the wall so she could peek around the corner.

She ignored Garyck's glare and spoke directly to me. "There's two guards posted in front of the door to the labs. And, big surprise, they're armed with laser pistols."

Vurell must still be alive. There was no reason for

armed sentries to be outside the lab unless there was something, or someone, inside they wished to prevent from leaving. I knew if we engaged the males directly, we would not be able to get close to the room without one of us getting injured. I rubbed my nape. "Is this the only entrance?"

"I'm afraid so." Laria tapped her chin. "Although, there is an air supply duct that runs along the ceiling. We could access the room that way. Then maybe we could draw the guards inside and disarm them."

"Do I want to know how you are aware of this system?" I asked.

"Sloane had a crush on one of the guys, er, males, who worked in the agricultural lab, so we…"

Sloane pinched Laria's arm. "I'm sure they're not interested in hearing about our teenage exploits."

Garyck's grunt earned him a glower from Sloane.

We headed back the way we came. Once inside the engineering tunnel again, Laria showed us the duct hidden behind a panel in the wall. After the cover was removed, Garyck held the glow emitter so we could see inside.

"The space looks pretty tight. Are you sure you guys want to go in there? Sloane and I can go and check out the lab."

"We will be fine." I appreciated her concern, but I was not letting her go anywhere without me, not when I didn't know what she'd be facing.

This time, Garyck did not have a problem letting Sloane lead the way. We crawled on our hands and knees through the tight space, an anxious twitch running along my tail. When we reached an area where the metal enclosure narrowed further, I was forced to skim the smooth surface on my belly. The fear of getting stuck was overridden by having Laria a hand's reach in front of me.

"Here it is." Sloane's whisper echoed back to me.

Fortunately, the duct in this area was considerably wider, providing room between my shoulders and the cold metal. By the time Laria and I reached Sloane and Garyck, they had scooted to the other side of a vented panel that covered the opening leading into a room.

"We can't see much from here. This vent accesses a storage alcove next to the lab," Laria said.

I leaned past Laria and peered through the thin metal slats. There was a large structure beam located on the left side of the vent, and she was correct—from this angle it was difficult to view the remainder of the room.

"The main area is around the corner to the right. If we enter here, we should be able to see what's going on without anyone seeing us." Laria retrieved a thin blade from her boot and used it to remove the vent covering.

Once she pushed the panel aside, Garyck moved in front of Sloane. "It is a long way to the floor. I will go first and catch you."

"What makes you think I can't get down there by myself?" Sloane huffed.

Garyck made one of his insistent grunts.

"Fine, but if you drop me, I'm going to kick your ass."

Garyck laughed. "Do not worry, little one. I will not drop you." He lowered his long legs through the opening. "I do not understand what is wrong with my backside or why you would want to kick it. But you are more than welcome to try any time you choose."

"It's a human saying. When we get back to the city, I'll be happy to give you a demonstration." Sloane patted his cheek before he dropped to the floor. She rolled onto her stomach, swung her legs out backward. "I mean it, Garyck" was all she said before disappearing from sight.

As much as I wanted to get out of the tight enclosure and find Vurell, I could not stop thinking about the interaction between Garyck and Sloane. It had been a very long time since I had heard my friend speak that many words in a single conversation.

Without my having to say anything to Laria, she moved and motioned for me to exit next. Once my feet touched the ground, she was already hanging over the edge, so I reached up and helped her the rest of the way down.

Silently, I moved ahead and headed in the direction that Laria said would lead to the main area of the lab. I heard noises and the mumble of a familiar male voice. With my hand on the hilt of my sword, I inched around the corner, glad to see that the room was free of any more guards. I spotted Vurell hovering near a table covered with various-sized glass containers, some filled with different colored liquids. There were also a variety of cylinder pots containing suclorra plants, which I knew were the source of the toxin.

His hair was mussed, some of the dark strands having escaped the tie at his nape. He did not appear happy with whatever he was working on. His brow appeared permanently etched into a frown. Next to him stood a young human male dressed in an oversized shirt, the hem stretching to the knees of a faded pair of baggy pants, the long sleeves rolled to expose a portion of his hands. Dirt smudged his face, and he wore an odd-looking piece of fabric that covered the back of his head, concealing his hair and a majority of his forehead. He saw us and froze, shock gleaming in a pair of dark eyes.

"Um, Vurell." The male nudged my friend, his gaze locked on Garyck and me.

Vurell jerked his head in our direction, first with a look of surprise, then disapproval. "Jardun, Garyck, what are you doing here?" His tone suggested he wasn't happy to see us, but his shoulders sagging with relief said otherwise.

He was five years my senior, an exemplary physician and a good friend. He was also a valued healer, one who had seen to my injuries on more occasions than I could count. A bruise marred his jaw, the skin beneath his eyes darkened from exhaustion. He'd obviously refused to do as Doyle had instructed and taken a beating for it. His arms were covered in injuries, some older and healing, some more recent. It appeared as if someone had peeled several of the scales from the skin on his arms.

I clenched my fists. The need to exact revenge on the humans who had done this to him replaced the relief I felt at finding him alive. "We came to take you home."

"You should not have come. We won't make it out of the vessel." Vurell's frantic gaze shot to a flat, rectangular black panel on the wall in a corner near the ceiling. "When the humans got the power to work, they also activated the ship's cameras. They have been monitoring my movements closely and will send guards once they realize you are here."

"Crap." Sloane shared a knowing look with Laria. "I forgot about the cameras."

No sooner had she made the statement than the door leading into the outside corridor retracted. Two males, presumably the ones Sloane had seen, walked into the room, each aiming a laser pistol in our direction.

"Well, look what we've got here. The doc has some new friends," Rick, the human male we had seen at the outpost, said with a sneer. "I was a little surprised that Burke didn't recognize me. I knew there was no way he'd be involved with one of the drezdarr's inspections. I guess Doyle was right when he said you'd be coming for the doctor."

"You know if Doyle decides to let us pass the women around, I call dibs on the pretty blonde." The male standing next to Rick licked his lower lip. He had been staring at the Laria and Sloane from the moment he entered the room.

I snarled, pushing Laria behind me at the same time Garyck took a protective step in front of Sloane. The male would die slowly if he touched her. I knew many ways to inflict pain with a blade that would not result in an instant death.

"Don't," Laria whispered, then squeezed my arm, urging me to ease my hand away from the hilt of my sword.

"You might want to listen to her," the other male said. "One shot from my weapon and you'll be dead before you reach the ground."

"Carl, go tell Doyle we found the rest of his uninvited visitors," Rick ordered, then grabbed the young male who had been working with Vurell and shoved him toward the doorway.

Carl paused in the corridor, casting a worried glance at Laria and Sloane.

"I said go." When Rick took a threatening step toward Carl, he didn't hesitate to disappear from view.

Rick returned his attention to us. "Take off your swords and put them on the counter, then take a seat against that wall over there." He motioned toward an empty space on the floor.

"What about the women?" Rick's friend asked.

"Until we know what Doyle wants to do with them, they can take a seat with the ketaurrans."

LARIA

I would've preferred a chair rather than having to sit on the cold metal floor with my back braced against the wall. The rest of the group didn't look particularly comfortable either. Garyck was sitting on Jardun's left with his elbows balanced on his knees, his angry glare never leaving Rick or the other male. I'd taken the spot on Jardun's right, with Sloane sitting next to me.

Jardun maintained his composure well, the twitch of his tail the only sign of his frustration.

"Stop worrying about your friends, Doc. You should be more concerned about what Doyle's going to do to you if you don't get back to work." Rick spoke from the other side of the room. He'd spent the last ten minutes or so with his back pressed against the frame of the open doorway, his attention periodically shifting from us to the outside corridor.

The other guard, whose name we learned was Neil, perched on the corner of a nearby worktable. Apparently bored, he passed the time by randomly picking up one of several vials filled with colorful liquids from a plastic rack sitting next to his hip. After holding the thin clear tube in the air and studying its contents, he'd return it to the stand and select another.

"We need to find a way to dispose of these human males," Garyck muttered.

"As long as they possess the laser weapons, there is little we can do." I was not willing to let anyone I cared about be injured or killed. All I could do was bide my time until an opportunity presented itself.

"Maybe you can't, but I can." Sloane pushed to her feet.

"Sloane, don't do it." I wasn't quick enough to grab my friend's arm and yank her back to the floor before she took several slow steps in Rick's direction. I knew exactly what she was planning to do. She'd done it before. During those instances, our opponents were armed with blades, something we were trained to battle. Not lethal laser weapons that could end a life with a simple blast.

Garyck growled and would have wrestled her back to the ground if Jardun hadn't grabbed his arm to stop him. I was glad Jardun had figured out what Sloane was planning to do without me having to say anything.

"Hey there, handsome." Sloane took a few more steps, adding an additional sway to her hips.

"You need to go sit back down." Rick pushed away from the frame and moved farther into the room.

"Nah, Rick, let her stay." Neil slid off the table, his interest piqued.

"Thanks. It's just that sitting on the floor is putting my ass to sleep." Sloane rubbed her right butt cheek for emphasis. "And I was getting bored."

"I'm sure we can find something to do to pass the time. Maybe you'd like me to give you a personal tour of the store room in the back." Neil lowered his weapon.

We didn't get a chance to find out if Sloane's plan to lure Neil away from Rick would work. The sound of loud coughing echoed through the room and drew everyone's attention to Carl, who was standing in the doorway.

Rick startled, then pivoted, his gun aimed at Carl's chest. "Damn it, kid. Don't you know any better than to sneak up on someone? I could've shot you." He aimed the weapon at the floor, then glanced at the empty corridor behind Carl. "What are you doing back here anyway? I told you to go find Doyle."

"Did." Carl shrugged, then sauntered between Sloane and Neil. He moved toward the table filled with vials and glass containers, absently running his finger along the edge of the cluttered surface.

"Well, what did he say? Is he on his way here?" Rick asked.

Carl made a noncommittal noise and shrugged again.

"Rick asked you a question." Neil lowered his pistol and fisted the sleeve of Carl's shirt.

In a graceful and swift move, Carl smacked his hand away, then grabbed one of the containers filled with a dark green liquid and smashed it over his head. Glass shattered, the liquid coating his hair and face. Whatever was in the container must have stung because Neil yelped and dropped his weapon, then frantically tried to wipe his face and eyes. Unable to see where he was going, he staggered backward and bounced off the table.

Some of the liquid had dripped on the floor, and when he caught it with his heel, he slipped and landed on his ass. Before Neil could get back up, Carl kicked him in the chest, the blow sending him the rest of the way to the floor.

Sloane used the distraction to yank the laser pistol from Rick's hand. No sooner had she leveled the weapon at his chest than the rest of us were at her side, ready to assist.

"Thanks." Carl winked, then stepped over Neil's

unconscious body and picked up his dropped weapon. After lifting her shirt, she tucked the gun in the back of her pants.

I couldn't figure out why Carl's voice sounded so familiar or why Sloane was staring at him as if he were a newly discovered life form.

Vurell joined us, his wide-eyed glance jerking from Neil to the young male. "Carl, why…how?"

"Vurell, I…"

"I knew it," Sloane interrupted, her lips widening into a beaming grin. "There's only one person I know who uses those sneaky moves." She threw herself at Carl, the force of the hug nearly knocking them both over.

I thought my friend had lost her mind until Carl giggled and returned the embrace. "Good to see you too."

"Little one, please explain." Garyck still looked like he wanted to throttle Sloane for her earlier actions. I couldn't blame him, I'd thought about choking her myself for trying something so reckless. "Do you know this male?"

"Not a male." Sloane snatched the knit hat from Carl's head, revealing a mop of short, dark chestnut curls.

"No way. Cara…how?" I mumbled, too shocked to form a complete sentence. I pulled her into a quick hug, a lot of questions rolling through my mind. Why she was wearing a dirty and smelly disguise was at the top of the list.

"You've been gone for months. I was afraid something had happened to you." I swallowed against the constriction in my throat. "That we'd never see you again."

"I know, and I'm sorry." Cara snatched the hat back and returned it to her head, tucking the loose curls inside. "When Burke heard there was a possibility that some laser weapons had been found, he asked for volunteers to infiltrate Doyle's compound. I wanted to tell you, but I couldn't. The fewer people who knew, the better my odds of getting the information we needed."

"Is that why you're dressed like a guy?" Sloane asked.

"These creeps will nail anything with breasts." Cara rolled her eyes in disgust at Rick, then kicked Neil's leg. "Pretending to be a guy was the only way I could keep from being forced to be someone's bunk partner. Most of the men ignored me, so it was easy to move around the ship without anyone getting suspicious."

She held up a hand. "I know you have more questions, but they're going to have to wait. Doyle has Burke and Celeste." She glanced at Jardun and Garyck. "And I'm assuming the ketaurran with them is one of your friends."

Jardun nodded. "Yes…Zaedon."

"Sorry, Cara. This is Jardun and Garyck." I pointed at each of them.

"Nice to meet you, but we need to go." The playfulness left Cara's voice. "I jammed the signal on the cameras, and it won't be long before someone comes to investigate."

"We cannot leave without the antidote," Vurell stated gruffly, then reached beneath one of the rectangular tables to retrieve a small insulated bag with a long strap.

"Fine, gather whatever samples you need while I lock Neil and Rick in the storage room," Cara said.

Hearing there was a cure and knowing we had a chance to save the drezdarr's life filled me with hope. Now the only problem we faced was getting the miraculous drug back to the city. I shared a concerned glance with Jardun before he followed Vurell across the room to help him select vials from one of the worktables.

Rick pursed his lips and glared at Cara. "Carl, or whoever you are, there's no way you'll make it out of here alive."

"We'll see. Now move." Cara shoved him toward the closed door in the corner of the room.

"Would you mind sharing those beefy muscles of yours and giving her a hand?" Sloane patted Garyck's arm and tipped her head at Neil's unmoving form.

"Pleasure." Garyck grabbed Neil by the ankle and dragged him effortlessly behind Cara. I couldn't tell if Neil banging his head on a table leg along the way was an accident or part of Garyck's plan. The ketaurran didn't seem bothered by it either way.

While Cara secured the lock, Sloane and I grabbed our swords, then checked the corridor outside the main entryway. So far, the passageway was empty.

"You guys ready to go?" Cara said once everyone had joined us. "Good, then follow me and stay close."

CHAPTER THIRTEEN

LARIA

Whoever was responsible for getting the power to work on the lab level also got one of the lifts working. After leading us to the end of the passageway, Cara shuffled us inside the convenient conveyor, which was a lot faster and easier to use than the engineering tunnels.

After finding the passageway on the new level empty, Cara motioned to her left. "Doyle took everyone to his office. It's down this corridor to the left. He only had one guard outside the room when I was scouting the area before. He's armed with a laser pistol, so we'll need to distract him."

"How do you propose we do that?" I asked.

Sloane grinned. "We could just shoot him."

"And I would agree with you if I wasn't worried that Doyle might still be inside the room with our friends." Cara held up a finger. "Wait here. I'll go around to the other side of the corridor." She winked and took another passageway. Unlike the layout on the lab level, this area was designed as quarters. Many of the corridors intersected, forming large squares in the layout. I always wondered if the architectural engineers who'd come up with the plan had purposely designed it that way to make getting around it easier or if it had been by accident.

A minute later, I heard Cara's voice, and peeked around the corner. The guard's weapon was still holstered to his waist, but his jaw was practically hanging on the floor. Cara had taken off her hat and tied the ends of her shirt into a knot around her waist, exposing a portion of her midsection.

"Carl, what the... You're a girl, but how?" Confused yet wary, he took an uneasy step toward Cara.

She sauntered closer to the male. "Correction, I'm a woman."

"I can see that." The suspicion in his tone was replaced with lustful appreciation. When he started moving closer, Cara spun, leveling her leg with a kick that landed in the center of his chest. He expelled a groan as he staggered backward and slammed into the wall. The back of his head bounced off the metal hard enough to daze him, and he dropped to the floor.

Before he could recover, Cara pounced, then rolled him onto his stomach with her knee pressed firmly against his spine. She removed his pistol and tapped his shoulder with it. "Where's Doyle? Is he still inside with the prisoners?"

"You can go fu..."

Cara cut off his words by grabbing a handful of hair and jamming the weapon into his neck. "Last chance."

The rest of our group had joined Cara and were waiting for the male to answer.

His hesitation was brief. "Said he was headed for the lab."

It was a good thing Cara hadn't chosen a direct route to reach this level of the ship. Otherwise, we would have run into Doyle. If the lab really was his destination, it wouldn't take long for him to figure out we were gone and where we'd headed. It also meant we didn't have much time to get our friends and get out of here. "Are there any other guards inside?" I asked as I drew my sword.

When the male took too long to answer, Cara tightened the grip on his hair. "No, only me."

Sloane already had the weapon she'd confiscated in the lab drawn and was reaching for the manual control on the door. After a quick glance inside, she gave Cara an acknowledging nod. "Celeste, are you…" Her voice faded as she disappeared into the room.

"Allow me," Garyck walked up to Cara. As soon as she released the guard, Garyck grabbed him by the back of the shirt, yanked him to his feet, then shoved him toward Doyle's office.

"Your friend is quite impressive. Does she match your skills with a sword?" Jardun hadn't been far from my side since we'd left the lab.

"Her friend prefers to use her fists and her feet," Cara said as she sauntered past them and headed inside the room.

By the size and interior design, this was one of the larger rooms on this level and, if I remembered right, was used as a meeting room by the ship's old commander and the council. The conference-sized table and the adjoining chairs were still bolted to the floor. The shelves running along one wall were filled with valuables, an assortment of items that had made the trip from Earth. Items I was sure hadn't originally belonged to Doyle.

"See if you can find something to tie him up." Cara directed her instruction to Garyck. "We don't need him sending out an alert before we get off the ship."

After glancing around the room, Garyck pulled back his fist and swung, the punch catching the male's jaw and knocking him out.

"Orrr that works," Cara said.

I was glad to see that Celeste was okay, but could have done without her excited shrill when she realized Carl was really Cara.

Other than a few scrapes, Zaedon didn't look too bad either. Burke, on the other hand, was in bad shape, most likely the result of an encounter with someone's fist. One of his eyes was swollen shut. He had a split lip, and his jaw was red with early signs that there would be bruising. The pants covering one thigh had been sliced, and blood coated the fabric. Sloane had already cut the ties binding his wrists to the chair and was fastening one of the longer lengths around his leg to slow the bleeding.

I tried not to wince. "Burke, I hope the other guy looks worse than you do."

Burke rubbed his wrists. "I wish. Doyle never was one to fight fair."

Garyck helped Burke to his feet, then draped one of his arms over his shoulders. Zaedon took a few steps closer to Cara, tugging a curl as if testing to see if it was real. He took several long sniffs, then wrinkled his nose. "The male who is a female smells worse than a pile of chaugwas dung."

"Zaedon, right?" Cara sneered and pushed his hand away.

"Yes." He quirked a curious brow, clearly surprised she was aware of his name.

"We don't have time to discuss my personal hygiene right now. It won't be long before the cameras come back online and the others come after us."

"Not to mention Doyle won't be happy when he discovers Vurell isn't in the lab," I added.

Celeste grabbed their sheathed swords from a nearby counter in a wall unit. She kept Burke's and tossed Zaedon's at him on her way to the outside corridor.

Doyle's room was located on the main level, which also happened to be close to the entrance at the front of the ship. Even with Burke's injury, it didn't take us long to make our way to the exit.

Jardun cautiously surveyed the area outside the vessel. "Where are the three males we saw earlier?"

"We took care of one of them. The other two accompanied Doyle," Zaedon said.

"Head for that solarveyor over there." Cara pointed at the largest of the transports. "The solars have been fully charged."

"And how would you know that?" Sloane asked.

Cara grinned. "It's amazing what you learn when no one pays any attention to you." She leaned against the exterior hull and aimed her laser pistol back inside. "Now, go. I'll catch up."

Zaedon stepped aside, withdrawing his sword as the rest of us passed. Cara wrinkled her nose at his blade, raising her gaze to his face. "They have guns. What do you think you're going to do with that?"

"Whatever is necessary to keep you safe." He moved to the opposite side of the opening.

"Ketaurrans," Cara muttered under her breath, then returned her focus to the dimly lit passageway.

I turned to stay with my friend, but Jardun grabbed my arm to stop me. "Where are you going?"

"I can't leave Cara behind."

"Zaedon will make sure she reaches the transport." He gave my wrist a gentle tug.

Cara was a stellar fighter. I didn't think Zaedon would appreciate hearing that it might be the other way around. I gave the two a frustrated glance, then groaned and paced alongside Jardun until we reached the transport.

Celeste and Vurell had helped Burke into a seat and were securing his safety strap. Sloane was hovering near one of the portals, her gaze focused on the ship. Garyck was in the control seat, his fingers flitting over buttons, the engine rumbling to life. He maneuvered the vessel as close to the ship's entrance as possible, moving slowly but not stopping.

I braced my feet on the floor and clutched a bar near the open doorway, ready to give Cara and Zaedon assistance. They were already under attack and running in our direction. Cara aimed her weapon behind her, firing shots to keep Doyle and his men from following. One of her shots hit the control for the main door, and it started to close.

When they were a few feet away, Zaedon grabbed Cara around the waist, then hoisted her up and followed her inside. "Go," I hollered at Garyck and hit the button to seal the door.

JARDUN

It must not have taken the humans long to get the main doors of the spaceship open again. I notice two of the solarveyors trailing behind us in the distance. Currently, they were too far away to catch us easily. Garyck was pushing our vessel to its limit, the hull vibrating, the whine from the engine's increased speed rippling through the interior. The additional speed we needed to outrun any pursuing vehicles would use the solarized energy reserves a lot faster than normal. I was not happy with our odds of making it out of the Quaddrien before the engines failed or we were overtaken by Doyle and his males.

I stared at the sunlight flickering through the clouds on the horizon, casting glints of green against the darkening backdrop of an impending storm, the rays too far away to come to our aid. If ever there was a time to hope that water wouldn't drop from the sky, it was now.

Zaedon was at my side, a disconcerted frown furrowing his brow. "You know they will not stop until they get Vurell and the antidote back and we are dead."

"I know," I said, glancing at Laria and her friends. Unless they tried to fight, I did not believe the females would be put to death. I did believe that dying would be a better end than what awaited them at the hands of Doyle and his males should we be overtaken. The thought of any male forcing his touch on Laria repulsed me and further fueled my resolve to prevent our recapture.

"I'm sure my destroying everything in the lab didn't help," Cara stated in a matter-of-fact tone.

"What are you talking about?" Laria asked.

I was curious as well. As far as I was aware, the female had done nothing besides secure the males in the storage room.

"When I jammed the camera signals, I set a timer to release the agent in the ceiling used to extinguish fires." Cara proudly cracked her knuckles. "That nasty foamy stuff has a long shelf life and is very potent. There's no way it didn't contaminate all the toxin samples. And yes, before you ask, I set it off in all the labs."

Knowing the mercenaries would no longer be able to replicate the toxin designed to kill my people provided me with a small amount of relief. It did not, however, assist with our current situation.

"This will work." Vurell approached from the rear of the transport, where he'd been rummaging through storage units. He smiled victoriously at the medical supply kit in his hands. He knelt in front of Burke and set the container on the bench next to him. Since leaving the lab, he'd kept the bag containing the vials strapped across his chest. Instead of removing it, he repositioned the bag so it pressed against his lower back.

"Can't this wait until we reach the city?" Burke grumbled.

"Only if you want to arrive without any blood left in your body." Vurell took the knife Celeste handed him and made a long cut in the fabric of Burke's pants.

"Don't be such a baby, Burke. Let the doc fix you up," Cara said.

"I'd hoped that spending time in the wastelands would've adjusted that impertinent attitude of yours." Burke hissed through his teeth when Vurell pressed on the skin around the gash.

"What attitude?" Cara chuckled. "I'm still the sweet-natured person I've always been."

"This is going to hurt." Vurell announced his warning at the same time he applied a liberal dose of an anti-infection herbal preparation. A preparation not known to possess soothing qualities.

"What the draeck, Doc?" If not for the safety strap holding him in place, Burke would have lifted off the seat.

It was comforting to know the time Vurell spent with Doyle had not changed his personality or the abrupt way he treated his patients. Vurell ignored Burke's complaints and wrapped a sealing gauze around the wound. "That will have to do until we reach Aztrashar." He closed the kit, then slid it in the empty compartment beneath an adjoining bench.

The transport rocked to the right as Garyck shifted directions to circle around the loicryn. Seeing the blur of blue as we rushed past the lush plant-filled area brought memories of my night spent with Laria. I glanced in her direction, noting the concern she held for her friends. If I had learned nothing else over the past few days, it was how precious the few gifts we received could be. She was one of those gifts, and it strengthened my resolve to do everything possible to keep her alive and in my life.

Laria must have gotten a glimpse as we passed and guessed the direction of my thoughts. She smiled, a hint of pink appearing on her cheeks.

"Hey, guys." Sloane had been kneeling on one of the benches near the rear of the vehicle and staring outside. "They're getting closer, so if you have any ideas on how we can slow them down, now would be a good time to share with the group."

"What about the snakkrils?" Laria asked.

Cara wrinkled her nose. "What the heck is a snakkril?"

"They're these snaky lizard creatures with huge fangs that live in the ground," Celeste answered. "Oh, and they're poisonous, as in you're dead after one bite."

"Yes, but they'll attack anything that moves if they think their offspring are in danger. If we drive near their nests, maybe we can use them as a distraction," Laria said.

I was reminded of the day before and how close I had come to losing Laria. Our situation was dire, we lacked resources, yet I had to admire her ingenuity for coming up with the solution, no matter how risky. There were very few areas along the rocky wall surrounding the Quaddrien where the terrain was low and level enough for a transport to travel. The site where we were attacked was out of our way, but not by much.

"Since we are aware of their location and the other males are not, it could work," Zaedon added.

Celeste shook her head. "Or we could end up being their next meal."

"What happens if they get underneath our vehicle and do something to the engine?" Sloane asked.

"They cannot get inside. The metal is too thick for their fangs or claws to penetrate," Zaedon said.

"These things have claws too?" Cara sounded more impressed than afraid.

"And if we get stranded?" Celeste pressed one hand to her hip. "Then what?"

"Look guys, I don't think we have much of a choice." Cara blew out an exasperated breath. "Doyle is one mean, crazy asshole, and his men aren't much better. Let's not forget that they're armed with laser pistols. One lucky shot to the solar drive…" She expanded her fingers to mimic an explosion. "…and we're done."

"I agree with Cara and say we go with Laria's idea." Burke fiddled with the latch, trying to free the strap keeping him in place.

"Where do you think you are going?" Vurell shoved Burke's hand away.

"If we end up in a fight, I won't be much good strapped to a seat," Burke said.

"You will not be of help if you move your leg and tear open your injury either."

"Here. Maybe this will help." Sloane retrieved the gun

she'd confiscated from Rick. She appeared reluctant to part with it when she handed it to Burke.

"Then it is agreed. We head for the nests." I searched the faces of everyone around, receiving affirmatives. Celeste did not seem convinced, but finally gave me a nod. "Garyck." I could have saved my breath. He was already manning the controls, the solarveyor vibrating with the abrupt shift toward our new destination.

CHAPTER FOURTEEN

LARIA

"Why did you tell Garyck to slow down?" Celeste pinned Jardun with an incredulous look, panic lacing her heightened voice.

My anxiety equaled my friend's. Slowing down as we approached the nest site hadn't been part of my plan. Skimming across the sand, waking the snakkrils, then making a speedy run for the nearest exit out of the wastelands had been what I'd envisioned.

"If we do not operate at a lower speed, then we will not have enough power to reach the Quaddrien's exterior border," Jardun said. "We also need the other transports to be close once we wake the snakkrils."

I'd been around Jardun long enough to know that he took his leadership responsibilities seriously. He would never willingly put any of our lives at risk without a good reason. I also didn't want to be trapped in the wastelands, not with Doyle's transports bearing down on us, and certainly not being this close to the snakkrils.

"I hope this works." Sloane hadn't moved from her kneeling position on the bench at the rear of our vehicle, nor had she stopped staring outside since everyone had decided to move forward with my plan. "Because they're right behind us."

I moved next to the viewing portal so I could get a better look. Sure enough, the other transports were getting a lot closer. "Where are they going?" The two vessels were moving farther apart from each other. Up until this point, they had stayed close and had been traveling in tandem.

"Crap." Sloane pushed off the seat, slipped between Celeste and me, and plopped down in the copilot seat next to Garyck. "You need to do something, or they're going to flank us."

Garyck released a threatening rumble but didn't increase the transport's speed.

"All right, stop growling. I'm doing it." Sloane snapped the seat's safety strap into place.

If we survived Doyle's attack and made it back to the city, I was definitely going to ask Sloane how she was able to understand what Garyck's various grunts meant.

"Everybody needs to hold on," Sloane called loudly over her shoulder.

I didn't have time to react before Jardun had his strong arm wrapped around my waist, pulling me tight against his chest. He steadied us by holding one of the horizontal support beams that ran along the interior wall with his other hand.

Vurell remained in the seat across from Burke, secured his strap, and kept a tight grip on the bag containing the vials sitting on his lap.

Celeste, Zaedon, and Cara were standing. To prevent being tossed around, they reacted quickly by latching onto bars similar to the one Jardun was gripping. When Garyck jerked the transport to the left, I clutched Jardun's shoulder.

My heart pulsed rapidly, and every nerve in my system was vibrating with anxiety. Part of it I attributed to our current situation; the rest I was certain was my reaction to being in Jardun's arms. An embrace that made me feel safe.

Jardun spoke over my shoulder to Zaedon and Garyck. "If they are able to overcome our vessel, we cannot allow Doyle to confiscate the antidote or take Vurell and the females."

"This female is quite capable of protecting herself, thanks." Cara flexed the fingers on her free hand.

Zaedon flared his nostrils and grinned. "You will not need to worry about fighting. After one whiff of your scent, the males will abandon your capture."

"Just for the record..." Cara sneered. "I'm not impressed with your sense of humor."

Zaedon chuckled, then returned to staring out the nearest pane.

The transport rocked, Jardun and I swaying with the motion. I could see the vehicle moving along our right. It was rapidly approaching and would soon be side by side with us.

"Laria." Jardun's deep voice rumbled in his chest.

"Yes?" I pulled my gaze away from the threatening sight outside to focus on his.

"If things go badly, promise me you will not do anything foolish." He pressed a kiss to my forehead. "I do not wish to lose you."

Was there a deeper meaning hidden behind his words and the piercing intensity of his blue-green eyes? Did his concern for my welfare go beyond the warrior's duty-bound honor to protect me because I was a female? Was it possible he secretly craved the same future I did, one where we were together and not apart?

I reached up and cupped his cheek. "The same goes for you." The possibility of a life with Jardun was all the incentive I needed to push aside my personal feelings and draw on my training, the instincts that helped me survive. I shifted my stance, turning to see past the panoramic view of the sprawling flat and sandy area in front of our transport. In the distance, I spotted the darkened outline of my chaugwas's carcass and knew we were getting close to the snakkril's nest. I didn't want another painfully vivid image of the dead animal to add to my mental collection, so I refrained from staring.

"What the draeck is Doyle doing?" Zaedon growled.

I glanced back through the side pane to see what had caught Zaedon's attention.

Burke hadn't been kidding about Doyle's level of insanity. The male had pushed the sliding door panel aside on his vessel. He stood in the middle of the opening, a tight grip on the frame. With a maniacal intent, he aimed the weapon in his free hand in our direction.

"He's going for the engine." Cara stuck her hand underneath her shirt and retrieved the laser pistol.

The blast hit the hull, the zing echoing through the interior, the vessel rocking as Garyck maneuvered away from Doyle's next attempt.

The two males piloting Doyle's transports had to be communicating with each other. The vessel on our left pulled ahead slightly, closing the gap, trying to force us closer to Doyle. When that didn't work, he rammed the side of his vessel into ours, adding the scrape of metal against metal to the air.

The spot where we'd been attacked by the creatures loomed in front of us. Garyck slowed the transport even more. The vehicle rebelled against the motion, the floor vibrating from the engine's whine.

"Garyck, what the…" Sloane might have been strapped in, but it didn't stop her from lurching forward and slapping her hands on the control panel in front of her.

I was glad I wasn't the only one who wanted to know what he was thinking. I changed my mind when I noticed Doyle's vessel's zoom past us, unprepared for the sudden maneuver. Garyck immediately banked hard to the right in order to avoid driving anywhere near a nest.

As soon as the other two transports slowed to turn and

follow us, a pit opened up in the ground and a snakkril sprang from the sand, wrapping its body around the front end of the transport that had rammed us. For once, luck was on our side, and so was my shock. "I can't believe it's working."

Even inside our vessel, I could hear the creature's unnerving shriek as it banged its head against the pane, trying to get to the males inside. It reminded me of my own near-death encounter and sent quivers skittering along my spine.

Cara had moved closer to me so she could get a better look at what was happening outside. "Wow, they can move fast." She shot Celeste a quick glance. "You weren't kidding when you said snaky lizards." She exaggerated a shudder. "Nasty-looking things."

A close-up image of long, deadly fangs popped into my head. "You have no idea."

Another hole opened up, exposing a creature larger than the first one, which I assumed was its mate. It slither-crawled toward Doyle's vehicle. From here, it looked as if Doyle was shouting commands and trying to get the door closed at the same time.

I silently cheered when the creature managed to get the upper portion of its body through the narrow opening. The males inside wouldn't be able to use their laser weapons, not without risking damage to the transport and its operating system. I hoped it did some major damage before someone got a chance to kill it.

Garyck had straightened out our vehicle, increased the speed, and was moving in a new direction. Jardun still had his arm around my waist. I lifted my head and asked, "Now what?"

He gave me a hesitant yet reassuring, smile. "Now we hope the snakkrils keep the other males busy long enough for us to leave the Quaddrien."

JARDUN

It was nearing nightfall by the time we reached Aztrashar. The strain the transport's engine had sustained was apparent in the uneven whirring and sputtering noises it made when Garyck forced it to stop in front of the drezdarr's dwelling. Even now, the gauges on the control panel indicated the vehicle's energy levels were close to depletion. Several times in the last few hours, Garyck had been forced to reduce our speed.

After barely escaping Doyle's transports, the time it had taken us to reach the outer border of the Quaddrien, then make the final trek into the city had not been ideal. At least we had not been stranded or forced to finish the journey on foot.

The relief at seeing our home was currently being overridden by my anxiety to find Khyron and make sure he was still alive. The transport had barely stopped before Vurell had the door open and was rushing inside the building, the bag containing the antidote clasped closely to his side. A few minutes later, Vurell's assistant, Kren, showed up to help Garyck take Burke to the physician's medical chambers to have the injury on his leg treated.

Once everyone else had exited the vehicle, I pulled Laria aside. I wanted nothing more than to drag her to my private quarters, place her on my bed, and show her how much she meant to me, then convince her she belonged in my life.

But now was not the time. Duty and the promise I had made to my friend came first. "Go with Zaedon and the others. Once I have seen to the drezdarr, I will find you, and we will talk." I cupped her cheek, hoping the gentle caress was enough to impart my overwhelming feelings for her and keep her from leaving.

She placed her hand over mine. "Go, take care of your friend. I'll wait."

I glanced at Zaedon, giving him an unspoken request to look after Laria and her friends. After receiving his nod of acknowledgment, I turned and hastened inside.

I did not wait for Khyron to grant me permission to enter after I knocked on the door to his sleeping chamber. He sat in the center of his bed, his upper body propped with pillows. His condition had worsened. The scales covering his chest and the pallor of his skin were now a dull gray.

Khyron winced. "I see your manners have not improved since we last spoke, but I am glad to see you."

It seemed as if the simplest movement, even smiling, caused my friend a great deal of pain.

I glanced around the room, wondering why the physician was not present and administering the antidote to Khyron. "Where is Vurell?" I did not hold back the anger in my growl. As much as I wanted my friend's health returned, that wish was surpassed by my need to return to Laria.

"Calm yourself. I am here." Vurell entered the room behind me. He was carrying a tray that contained a glass filled with a light green liquid, along with one of the vials he'd retrieved from the lab in the human spacecraft. He placed the tray on the corner of Khyron's desk.

I ignored Vurell's sarcasm and returned my attention to Khyron. "I assume once you have recovered, you will want an update on our travels." I moved closer to his bed, intent on staying by his side as long as he needed me. "There are things of importance we need to discuss." The events surrounding the males at the outpost was at the top of the list.

"Such as?" Khyron coughed.

"They will have to wait," Vurell interjected, then poured the contents of the vial into the liquid.

Khyron bowed his head at Vurell, then spoke to me. "As will introductions to our human guests. Please give them my apologies." His cough was much worse this time, and he pressed a hand to his chest. "There are complications with my recovery."

I glared at Vurell. "Is something wrong…with the antidote?" The thought of losing Khyron after everything my friends and I had done to save him caused the muscles in my chest to tighten.

"No," Vurell said. "Khyron's condition has progressed to an advanced stage. I believe at this point, the curing potion I have developed will cause him extreme pain." He held up his hand to stop my argument. "I have prepared a drug that will induce sleep while he heals."

"How long must he slumber?" I asked.

"The effects will last several days, but after that, he should recover quickly." Vurell's emotionless features did not ease my trepidation.

"In the meantime, please inform Burke and the females that I insist they stay and make themselves at home."

Insisting was Khyron's way of stating an order, a mandate to be followed without question. It did not matter if Laria and her friends were human, they were required to adhere to ketaurran law and any orders issued by the drezdarr.

I was elated. Whether Khyron meant to or not, he had provided me with more time to convince Laria to stay.

"I want to thank them personally for the risks they took to save my life once I awaken." Khyron furrowed his brow at me. "Why are you grinning? Does my request amuse you?"

"I believe Laria is my ketiorra, and if she is required to stay…"

"You can entice her to agree to bond with you," Khyron finished for me.

"Yes." I widened my grin even more.

"Human females are unique…special."

I had seen that sad far-off look in Khyron's eyes on two other occasions. I knew he was thinking about the human female he believed was his ketiorra. I did not know her name, but knew he had lost her when Sarus's males attacked her settlement during the war.

"If she truly is your mate, then I am happy for you." He paused to take a breath. "It is time for change. With all the losses our people have suffered, there is no reason why the vryndarr should spend the remainder of their lives alone, without a female to share their future with."

"Zaedon voiced a similar viewpoint," I said.

"Perhaps these female warriors are the answer to breaching the gap between the humans and ketaurrans."

Vurell groaned. "Might I suggest you postpone plotting your grand plans until later? If I do not administer the antidote soon, you will not be around to interfere with everyone's future."

Khyron's laugh caused another bout of coughing. "It is apparent your ordeal in the Quaddrien has not dulled the sharpness of your tongue."

"It is one of the qualities that makes me an admirable physician," Vurell smugly replied.

"If not a cantankerous one," I teased, taking a few steps closer to the doorway and away from Vurell's reach should he decide to retaliate.

"I will show you cantankerous the next time you have an injury in need of repair." Vurell straightened his shoulders. "Now leave and let me see to the drezdarr's needs."

I grinned, then spoke to Khyron. "I expect to see you in a few days, so heal quickly."

CHAPTER FIFTEEN

LARIA

I'd promised Jardun I wouldn't leave, but waiting with nothing to do was not one of my strengths. The uncertainty that came with knowing he wanted to talk wasn't helping the condition of my frazzled nerves. If he was going to say goodbye, I wished he would've done it when we'd arrived. It wouldn't have spared me from suffering through the pain of a broken heart, but it would've been easier to walk away, to get on my transport and never look back.

I tried not to pace, but it had been hours since Zaedon had shown us to the same quarters we'd used the last time we were here. None of the males, including Jardun, had made an appearance. There weren't any guards posted in the corridor, a sign we'd earned the drezdarr's trust. The only person I'd seen after taking a bath and changing into clean clothes was a young ketaurran female who timidly left a tray of fruits and beverages before hastening from the room.

It wasn't helping that Celeste, Sloane, and Cara hadn't been bothered by the situation. They seemed perfectly content to relax and enjoy the accommodations.

"Do you think the drezdarr made it?" Sloane asked, making herself comfortable on one end of a lounger with her legs stretched across its length.

"After everything we did, he darn well better have survived." Cara reached for another piece of fruit and popped it into her mouth.

She was a few inches shorter than me, and the clothes I'd loaned her were a little baggy and wrinkled from being stuffed in my bag. She hadn't minded and was glad to be cleaned up and out of her grimy, smelly disguise.

"The drezdarr is alive." Hearing Jardun's deep voice had me spinning to face the doorway. He smiled, his gaze never leaving mine as he entered the room with Zaedon and Garyck following close behind him.

I spared a glance to notice they'd all taken the time to bathe and change before returning my attention to Jardun. His hair hung over his shoulders, the dark strands damp and glistening.

"He sends his regrets and asks that you remain his guests until he has completed his medical treatment," Jardun said.

Celeste sat forward and crossed her arms. "Is that his polite way of saying we aren't allowed to leave?"

"He wants to thank everyone personally and appreciates your compliance with his request."

I had to give Jardun credit for his tactful response and the way he'd addressed the drezdarr's order. An order we'd have to follow unless we wanted to end up in a holding cell. What made things even more uncomfortable was thinking about being trapped in the same building with Jardun if our discussion ended with us parting ways.

I could tell by the way Celeste narrowed her eyes and pursed her lips that an argument was about to ensue. "How's Burke doing?" I asked, hoping the interruption would keep my friend from doing anything that could cause us all problems.

“Other than arguing with Vurell, he is doing fine,” Zaedon said as he moved to stand behind Cara’s chair. He leaned forward and sniffed.

“What?” Cara shot him an over-the-shoulder glare and waved him away. “If you tell me I still smell like chaugwas dung, you’re going to be picking yourself up off the floor.”

Jardun held his hand out to me. “As much as I would be entertained to see you best my friend, I wish to speak to my ketiorra privately.”

Shock didn’t come close to describing my reaction. I forced myself to breathe. I couldn’t decide if I was angry he’d shared the information, or elated he was claiming me as his mate.

“I knew it.” Sloane’s overly enthusiastic smirk pushed me toward irritation first.

“You can’t tell everyone I’m your ketiorra without having some kind of discussion about it with me first.”

The flash of pain in his eyes, as if I’d wounded him with one of my blades, was quickly masked. “Are you saying you refuse to acknowledge our connection?” He curled his fingers and lowered his hand, but remained where he was.

“No, I’m saying it would have been nice to talk about it before sharing the information with everyone.” I slapped my hands on my hips, then glanced around the room, noting that our friends weren’t even bothering to hide their amusement.

Jardun stepped closer, caressing my chin with his thumb, drawing my attention back to him. “We did have a discussion.” He lowered his voice, his tone soothing.

“When?” The more he rubbed my skin, the less irritated I became.

“The night we stayed in the loicryn.”

“That was not a discussion. That was…” I recalled quite clearly what we were doing the moment he’d called me his ketiorra, and everything that happened afterward.

Jardun quirked a challenging brow.

"Oh."

"Do you wish to argue further?" Jardun asked.

"No, I'm done."

"Good, because I wish to have the remainder of our talk in private."

I didn't get a chance to do anything but squeal when I found myself lifted off the ground and draped over his shoulder. I might have verbalized a complaint if I wasn't so busy admiring his nicely muscled ass and the way his smoothly scaled tail swished back and forth as he carried me out of the room.

He was halfway down the corridor before I was hit by the reality of how my life was about to change. "Jardun, what about my friends?" I wanted a future with him, but not at the cost of giving up the people I considered family, or what we did for a living.

"They will be adhering to the drezdarr's order." He turned down another corridor. "Do not worry. Zaedon and Garyck will make sure they are well cared for."

"That's not what I meant."

He stopped long enough to open a door and walk into a dimly lit room. From this angle, I got an upside-down glimpse of a large bed, the frame carved from stone, and the opening to a terrace beyond.

He lifted me off his shoulder, my body sliding against his until my feet touched the floor, his hands remaining on my hips. "I wish for you to be by my side always, but I would never ask you to part from your friends."

The pounding in my chest increased, reality tightening its grip on my heart. It didn't matter how much I wanted to be with him; the fact that we lived in different worlds was never going to change.

He tucked my hair behind one ear, then cupped my cheeks. "I do not completely understand the human belief in fate, but I do believe we are meant to be together."

I closed my eyes briefly, savoring the warmth of his skin against mine. "But how? My life is back at the settlement, and yours is here with the other vryndarr."

He offered me a reassuring smile. "The drezdarr believes that all of us, the vryndarr and your friends, hold the key to healing the conflict between our people."

I placed my hand over his. "Really? What did he say?"

"He was unable to provide me with details, other than to say he would explain his plan to all of us after his treatment." He grabbed my ass and lifted me off the ground. "Now, my ketiorra, I plan to connect with you properly." He nipped the side of my neck. "I am certain the process will take several days."

I giggled and wrapped my legs around his waist. I knew exactly how he planned to connect, and if I had any doubts, the hard cock rubbing against the sensitive spot between my legs was a great indicator of his intentions. I smiled and pushed away my worries.

Whatever changes, obstacles, or dangers we encountered, I knew with all my heart that we'd be facing them together.

ABOUT THE AUTHOR

Rayna Tyler is an author of paranormal and sci-fi romance. She loves writing about strong sexy heroes and the sassy heroines who turn their lives upside down. Whether it's in outer space or in a supernatural world here on Earth, there's always a story filled with adventure.

Made in United States
Troutdale, OR
11/19/2023

14723348R00108